THE

THE MEGAROTHKE

ROBERT ASHCROFT

CINESTATE

CINESTATE.COM
@CINESTATEMENT
DALLAS, TX

The Megarothke
Copyright © 2018 by Robert Ashcroft

ISBN 9781946487063 *(paperback)*
ISBN 9781946487070 *(e-book)*

Library of Congress Control Number: 2018932279

Published by Cinestate
www.cinestate.com
Dallas, Texas

DESIGN & LAYOUT ASHLEY DETMERING
TYPESETTER KIRBY GANN
COPYEDITORS MOLLY WOLCHANSKY & FRANCIE CRAWFORD
DISTRIBUTOR CONSORTIUM BOOK SALES & DISTRIBUTION
EDITOR WILL EVANS
PRODUCER & PUBLISHER DALLAS SONNIER
AUTHOR ROBERT ASHCROFT

First Edition February 2018

Printed in the United States of America

ACKNOWLEDGEMENTS

First, I'd like to thank my parents. They've put up with a lot for my sake, and they've been real champs.

Second, I'd like to thank my good friend Ethan Cramer, who read three different versions of *The Megarothke*, as well as several failed manuscripts, countless short stories, and offered an enormous amount of feedback. Not only that, but he also generously allowed me to use the line, "Why do they bleed from their eyes?" from a role playing game he had previously created.

I'd also like to thank the entire Harker Heights Writing Group: Alex Burt, Sandra Desjardins, Kat Wooley, Andrea McCauley and Mark Crawford. Your weekly encouragement nursed this book to its final form.

In the end, none of this would have been possible without the faith and financial backing of Cinestate, specifically Will Evans and Dallas Sonnier. There's really no way to thank them adequately in this small space. These people take stories and give them wings; they risk their time, money, and reputation on every shot.

"Debut novelist Ashcroft unleashes a witch's brew of macabre, Lovecraft-ian imagery in this strange horror novel that couches a heavy emotional arc within its video game–like setting... It's some heavy mythology-building but Ashcroft's skillful blend of noir vocabulary and cyberpunk aesthetics work to its advantage. Between its robotic doppelgängers, mutated monsters, and actual ray guns, the book manages to take a hard look at what it means to be human in an age when humanity barely remains. A bloody, blistering novel of war and sacrifice set in a time of actual monsters." —**Kirkus**

Table of Contents

PART ONE

I tell you: one must still have chaos in one, to give birth to a dancing star.
I tell you: ye still have chaos in you.
—THUS SPOKE ZARATHUSTRA

1

SANTA MONICA COLLECTIVE
07/06/2051 (HW7)

Question: Where did the fiends come from?
Answer: The limitless depths of the Hollow War.

THE DOORWAY IN FRONT OF ME WAS IN BAD SHAPE. Only one hinge was left, and it was bent like a broken neck. The deadbolt had been ripped from the frame, and the metal handle lay down at my feet. Keeping my Vortex 19 raised and ready, my arms shook with exhaustion. For a brief, foolish second, I closed my eyes, and in that moment, I realized that Takatoshi had turned off his vision-sync again.

"Tosh—turn on your vision-sync," I said, a tense wave of dread coursing through my veins.

Takatoshi had been turning it off lately; said two sets of the things we saw were too much. We'd stopped by an old tech center during an extended patrol route and found a body hanging in the foyer. The body had been a member of the lost Anaheim Reconnaissance Squad. A sign had been pinned to his ribcage with pieces of broken rebar.

THE WORLD HAS BEEN REBORN.

That was all it had said.

The officer's face had been carved into a smile, and his dog tags had been jammed into his teeth.

Seven years before, the entire world outside of Los Angeles had been leveled by a massive, orbital rail-gun system. Within months of being spared by the initial blast, strange new breeds of creatures had descended from the hills and deserts of Southern California to feast upon the remaining population. Fiends, huddlers, bruisers: we called them the Scourge, as if they were one thing, but the only thing they had in common was a desire to wipe out what was left of humanity. By now, there were only around 50,000 of us left in Los Angeles.

Sure, it was possible there were a few other tiny cities left, scattered around the world. Even a coldly distant, almost mythically celebrated Orbital where Russian and Japanese billionaires had managed to flee. The consensus was that we needed to reach out, to connect, but we had to take care of our own problems first. There is a stage after tragedy where no one wants to talk about the past or look to the future. Call it a state of societal mourning.

"Takatoshi," I said, "Turn it back on."

Without response, Takatoshi turned his vision-sync back on. The screen appeared in the bottom left corner of my vision-field. I breathed a sigh of relief and re-gripped the Vortex. How long had it been since I'd slept?

"Theo," he said, his voice pointed away from mine, his Vortex also raised and sighted at the center of his vision, "You trust Aria?"

I kept my eyes on the door. This was no time for a discussion.

But the topic hit close to home.

"Sure," I said, "Why not?"

Silence. It was raining outside. A rare occurrence now, thunder sounding off in the distance. The invasive bone-stalks would be drinking it up like bamboo; the tuberous shoots grew everywhere, strangling the bushes and trees, sprouting from ventilation ducts and sewer drains.

I tried to take a deep breath while still holding my weapon trained. I thought about the body hanging there. I wanted to cut down the chain, identify him and give him a proper burial, but I knew it was futile, this far from the clusters. There was a good chance that we were standing at full attention in a very empty building. There was a good chance that the worst we would see for the rest of the day was an old, dyspeptic printer, left over from the bygone era, when quaint little machines didn't have cell-structures.

But then there was always still a small chance that whatever had strung the body up was still there. Perhaps even watching us. Waiting for that weak, human moment.

"She wants me dead," Takatoshi said. "Aria and Clark both do."

A shadow moved beyond the door. A chill ran up my spine.

"That's a negative," I said.

The drop ceiling above us creaked and groaned with the change in pressure from the storm outside. A few of the old fluorescent lights still flickered and hummed. The whole building was going through the first tremors of resurrection after years of disuse.

"Clark is helping her out," Takatoshi said. "They're going to feed us to the Recluse in exchange for another year of peace, and he's going to offer us up to the Megarothke. As sacrifices."

Stepping forward, toward the door, I tried to shake off the feeling that we were being watched.

"Wait," Takatoshi said.

I stopped.

The shadow flickered in front of the doorway again.

"You see that shadow?"

"Yeah," I said.

"Listen," he said, "None of us are going to make it out of here alive, in the long run."

I waited, listening to the rain.

"So just know this—we die with honor. If you're down with a bullet to the stomach, I'm putting another one in your head."

I closed my eyes in exhaustion. Again, a foolish move.

"Thanks," I said. I knew he meant it in the sincerest way possible. Obsessed with the sanctity of the past, Takatoshi hadn't so much as even told me his first name. Even Aria didn't know it. He'd said that when his family had died, he'd buried it with them.

"Tosh," I said.

Silence. He was waiting for me to continue.

"I'm not dying," I said. And with that, I took another step forward.

Two steps from the door, the whole room shook with a deafening explosion. Fluorescent bulbs swung from their racks, ceiling panels snapped in two, and an old ventilation duct came crashing down onto one of the desks.

Crouching, I spun in through the doorframe, ready to fire. The room was empty, but the door at the other end was open. Taking off in a dead sprint, I watched as Takatoshi's screen hustled to follow.

The next room was cluttered with old monitors, dust covered headsets with foam-tipped microphones still on their racks. The window on the far side of the room had been smashed out. Rushing to the window, I saw the fiend sprinting on all fours down the back alley.

Four shots. Fast. On target.

At least one bullet connected just to the left of the creature's raised spine. For a brief moment, the fiend lost its footing and glanced back. With a twist of its long neck, it stared right back at me—mottled yellow eyes framed by a thick, wolfish skull and blood-stained maw. In that split-second, I felt a hatred trained upon me that could scarcely be fathomed.

The bent posture and hock-jointed legs belied the fiend's nearly seven-foot stature; its hideous lupine face hid a feral intelligence that had grown sharper by the season.

Takatoshi entered the room just as my gun was going off, and kept his dead sprint going as he shouted, "Keep firing till I get there!"

I unloaded several more rounds at the creature, which was now bleeding and limping at a much slower pace. Dark red blossoms had already begun to form along the fur of its torso. By the time Takatoshi made it to the alley, a long trail of blood had been laid along the asphalt.

Taking the door that Takatoshi had found, I watched his vision screen in my peripheral as I came up along the side of the building.

From within the small green square, the creature turned, stood to its full height, and fired off three shots. Takatoshi went out like a light.

My heart stopped as his vision-sync went static.

Fuck!

As I turned the corner, I saw my partner pushing himself up. The creature was out of sight. There were no exit wounds on Takatoshi's back, so I knew he hadn't been hit with any sort of pulse weapon. In fact, I was pretty damn sure he hadn't been hit at all. As I grabbed his arm to pull him to his feet, he swore and wiped the blood from his chin with the back of his tactical glove.

"It had a gun! It had a *fucking* gun!"

The front of his trench coat was fine, a little wet from the rain, but there were no new bullet holes. The blue SMC Patrol armband over his left bicep had shifted, but not so much that people would confuse him for a refugee. The only blood present was from the trail of thick drops along the asphalt.

Seeing that Takatoshi was okay, I continued down the

alley, following the blood until it stopped at a gap that had been blown in the cinderblock wall. The gap led to the shallow backyard of a small ranch house. The ThermaGuard siding had been ripped off in a crude attempt to patch the windows, and the door hung halfway open.

Ducking behind the wall, I reloaded a fresh clip. Takatoshi came up alongside me and took a quick glance through one of the broken blocks. Bone-stalks had grown all around the sides of the house, some of them pushing under the boards and then emerging again like curious serpents. The house was silent.

"This shit isn't supposed to be happening up here," he said.

Leveling his gun with the hole, he fired seventeen shots in rapid succession. A flick of his thumb popped out the clip and he jammed in another. Seventeen more shots.

I turned on my knees and looked through a gap at the edge of the jagged wall. He was pounding the area below one of the windows. In between shots, I heard movement, and then a thud-crack, as if someone had fallen and knocked over a chair.

Takatoshi reloaded again.

We waited.

I pressed a button on my wrist-control to launch a sensor camera and activated a countdown in our vision fields.

100, 99, 98, 97, 96 . . .

The sensor camera was a mirrored sphere that would be shot from a rail-launch system in Buena Park all the way to the ocean. Every three months, we'd send a team out to the abandoned beaches, fish the camera balls back up, and load them right back into the shoots.

Takatoshi got up, but I put my arm out to stop him.

"We're following protocol," I said. "Let command run the sweep. I'm not walking into a trap."

He stared at me, sweat dripping down the sides of his face. His dark purple hair was brown at the roots, and while I had often wondered if he were only half-Japanese, it wasn't something I was going to ask him. Hell, like I said, I didn't even know his first name.

"Theo, what the hell is going on out there?" Aria snapped in her prudish tone. Beaming in from headquarters, her voice sounded extra sharp as it poured in through our recycled cochlear implants.

"We caught a fiend trapped in the old tech center," I said. "Do we have any results yet?"

"He had a *fucking* gun!" Takatoshi snapped.

"Are you okay?" she asked.

"We're good. I think we have the fiend trapped in an abandoned house," I said.

"He had a *fucking gun!*" Takatoshi snapped again.

"All right, the sensor-camera is sending back the imagery now. Looks like the burbs are clear of explosives, no large heat sigs to speak of . . ." she said. Then after swearing a few times under her breath, she continued, "There's nothing there to worry about, other than a herd of bruisers a few miles away. The house looks clean of ordnances anyway. Hold off until it's finished transmitting and then do a physical sweep. The fiend might still be around, and if we can't keep Anaheim at a yellow, then we may have to concede the entire area."

I sighed in exhaustion, yet again, and nearly collapsed.

"We'll check the house as soon as our count-down ends," I said. The timer was on 36.

"Copy," she said.

"Copy," I repeated.

"Ten-four," Takatoshi said, falling backward against the wall and sliding down to a sitting position.

We both rested. From my spot on my knees, I brought

myself down onto the back of my boots. Takatoshi wiped his forehead. I checked the magazine in my Vortex 19.

18.

17.

"Hey, Theo," Aria said.

My back straightened and my head shot up. Takatoshi looked over at me, ready to spring into action.

12.

11.

10.

"Be careful," she said.

Takatoshi looked at me and said, "What's up? What do you see?"

I shook my head. She'd called in through my private channel.

5.

4.

3.

Somewhere out in the Pacific Ocean, down south of Laguna Beach, a lonely sensor-camera plunged into the ocean.

2.

1.

"Transmission complete," Aria said, back in dispatcher-mode. "You're clear to enter."

"You ready to move in?" Takatoshi said.

"Always," I said, and then bounced back to my feet.

Following our leapfrog pattern, I laid down cover as Takatoshi sprinted and then dove down next to the wall. Then, jumping to his feet, he fired another clip into the window as I ran up to the side door. We covered the room as we entered, and then swung around to the bedroom with the boarded window.

Turning to cover him, I kept my gun on the living room

and what appeared to be the bathroom door.

But then I realized my back was blind.

"Tosh, your vision-sync," I called.

No response.

"Tosh, your vision-sync," I called again.

Only a hacking, gurgling sound.

Fear shot through my back, but I couldn't turn around. He should have had his VS on, and if I turned, I'd be leaving our back wide open.

"Takatoshi!" I shouted, "*Turn on your fucking vision-sync!*"

And then, in the confusion, I heard what sounded like vomiting coming from behind me, followed by a deep, emotion-filled inhalation. The type that sucks air through your vocal cords right down to the core of your being.

Glancing behind me, I turned and swung into the room.

Takatoshi was on the floor. On all fours. Vomit spilled in front of him.

And in the closet, with her back turned toward us, was a seven-year-old girl with a bullet through her head and several around her spine and rib cage.

Blood seeped down the wall and pooled in the carpet. A chair had fallen into the closet door, apparently knocked over as she had tried to duck into hiding. The fiend was nowhere in sight. It was probably miles away, dying in an alley.

My gun hung like a lead brick. My body stood only by virtue of my locked knees and poor posture. My world clouded over.

"It was a kid," Takatoshi said. "I put thirty rounds into a room with a little kid."

Taking a deep breath, I gathered myself. I'd lost a daughter in the Hollow War. I'd lost more than I cared to think about. But there was something wrong with the picture here. I took a step forward, toward where she lay.

The girl's skull was bloody, but it looked like a carbon-fiber shell had been cracked open under the bone. Walking toward the closet, I bent down for a closer look. The blood pooling in the carpet smelled like iron, and the coagulated darkness mixed with hair around the edge of the wound made my stomach turn. A loose shock of the girl's golden blonde hair stuck out, as if she'd been sleeping just before the shots.

Taking another step forward, I bent in closer still, eyes fixed on the peculiar curl crimped in the single shock of hair. It was as if it had been combed and hair-sprayed stiff, and then bent in the opposite direction. Like doll's hair. The rays of light from the bullet holes in the wall and window caught in the bent lock and made it appear dry and lifeless.

Then, with my breathing stabilized, I took a final step forward, crouched on the balls of my feet, and leaned in, less than a foot or so away.

The girl's torso jerked around with a single, violent motion. The swivel of her upper-body happened so fast that her delicate shoulders slammed back against the hollow wall with a force that cracked the sheetrock. The whole wall shook. Turned toward me now, her eyes cast a blank stare. One of them had filled with blood, but I could see now what I'd missed before.

With her torso and upper-body now facing away from her waist, it was far easier to see the subtle, designer curves of her facial features, still frozen in place even after death.

The button nose, the dimpled cheeks, the slender neck, the long lashes.

"It's okay, Tosh," I said, turning and grabbing the shelf to support myself. "You didn't kill a kid."

Takatoshi had pushed himself up on his knees, and was staring at the girl in the closet. With a pneumatic hiss, her jaw fell slack and steaming black oil flowed out over her teeth and lips, dribbling from her chin down onto her shirt.

This was a game changer. A harbinger. A black flag on the horizon.

I closed my eyes for a long time, not wanting to open them ever again. My eyes could stay closed forever, for all I cared. Like any of it was worth looking at anymore.

But then, in the bottom left corner of my vision, a green screen appeared.

Takatoshi had finally turned vision-sync back on.

2

BRUISERS

S O, HAVE YOU SEEN CLAUDIA LATELY?" I ASKED, TRYING to break the funk that had descended upon Takatoshi. Steering our patrol car with one palm, I curved through the husks of old self-driving cars and abandoned barricades while keeping a high visual horizon. The suburbs swum around us on gentle sloping hills.

This was our inheritance: crumbling asphalt roads between houses with cracked paint, broken windows, and sagging fascia boards. Barren lawns with leafless husks of trees. The only signs of natural life were the jointed, rib-like curves of pale, wet bone-stalks. They wrapped themselves around fence posts and burst from holes in the roofs like limp tentacles. We'd managed to set up greenhouse farms, but everything beyond the meticulously cultivated fell away—as if the earth were sloughing its skin.

Takatoshi still hadn't answered.

I thought again about the little girl we'd shot—how she was laid out in the trunk in a body-bag. More flesh than robot, but enough bio-tech to scare my imagination into a half-dozen different scenarios of her rising from the dead.

Back before the Megarothke had disappeared, the spies had infiltrated even the inner-most circles of the Santa Monica Collective. Our purging process had been brutal and improvised: x-rays, arm-cuts, blood samples, written tests, verbal interviews. The process was only several months from completion when the Megarothke Death Cults committed mass suicide and all coordinated activity ceased.

Since then, the Scourge had been a disorganized mess, more akin to wild animals than an invasion. If anything, they were led by the Recluse at this point, but the fact was we didn't really know.

I wanted to believe that the girl was just a malfunctioning unit. I wanted to believe anything other than the worst possible truth: that the Megarothke was back.

"Hey, Tosh, you seen Claudia lately?" I asked for the second time.

"I said, '*I don't know,*'" Tosh snapped back.

"Did you? Cause I didn't hear a goddamn thing," I matched his tone. I wasn't exactly in a great mood either.

"What does it matter? Why are you so curious all the sudden?"

Tosh was talking directly out the window, away from me.

"I was thinking that you might help her apply for permanent status at Buena Park," I said.

"She's not my girl," Takatoshi said. "She's just a refugee. I *had* a family, remember?"

A refugee. There were seven clusters in the Santa Monica Collective, which was all that was left of Los Angeles, which was all that was left of the world. Seven stars in the constellation of civilization. Over the years, we'd had a steady trickle of drifters and stragglers, but even those had tapered off lately.

By my guess, we had about 50,000 people in total. About

30,000 were official citizens of the SMC, and the rest were refugees that couldn't live within the walled clusters until they'd proven themselves useful and undergone full scans to make sure they weren't spies for the Recluse.

"I saw Claudia talking to Clark," Takatoshi said.

I waited.

"So?" I asked.

"Don't be a fool, you know what that means."

Clark abused refugees. This was common knowledge. Clark was the Superintendent of the Buena Park Cluster. As one of the seven Superintendents, he was essentially Duke of our little fiefdom of apartment buildings and climate controlled farming areas. When the Santa Monica Collective had established its power, they'd been very careful to give out the most harmless titles possible. Secretaries. Superintendents. Ministers.

"You don't want bad things to happen to her. Admit that, at least," I said.

Up ahead, another body hung from an old street light. The flesh looked as if it had rotted away months ago and its human shape was really only retained by the visor-less motorcycle helmet and shoulder pads. The body armor must have been linked together all the way down to the boots. We were farther east than we normally went and things were looking more ominous by the block.

I stopped the car and aimed at the chain that had been wrapped around the overhang in the streetlight. With one well-placed shot, the link snapped and the corpse fell to the pavement with a tired slap.

"Nice shot," grumbled Takatoshi, leaning forward to look at where the corpse had landed. "And listen, if Claudia's talked with Clark, there are only two possibilities. She'll get citizenship status and move in next to his apartment, or she'll disappear."

"Unless you talk to her first," I said. "Warn her. Guide

her. Etcetera."

"Fuck it. What's the use?"

"I mean, you don't want her to end up . . . you know?"

"Listen Theo," Takatoshi said. "We're all dead in the end; a bunch of chattering skulls, rickety skeletons parading about building castles on a planet that will one day return to dust."

I took a deep breath and held it. A way of not saying anything.

These death rants were simply Takatoshi's way of dealing with it.

Mine was guarding the secret. The secret I'd long buried. The secret that could not possibly be true. If the secret *were* true, then I'm not sure I would have been able to face another day. But it wasn't. So who cares? It wasn't true. I just couldn't tell anyone, either way.

As we curved around the hilltop, a fence that had collapsed under the weight of the alien foliage gave us clear sight of the valley below. I braked to a stop and killed the lights instinctively.

A low mist had settled amongst the fresh rubble of flattened houses and strip malls. A herd of bruisers blocked the path. Thousands of them. The acrid, astringent stench of their salivary dispensation assaulted us through the open car windows. Neither I nor Takatoshi said a word.

Like bison, but nearly fifteen feet tall and covered in a metallic chitin that caught in the setting sun, they moved slowly, stopping only to growl and spray an acidic secretion from under their forelimbs over the piles of rubble. This solution allowed them to chew through the concrete and metal, scooping up jaw-fulls of the 21st century with each bite. The thick metal plating along their foreheads let them work like mobile wrecking balls, reducing entire business complexes to rubble within the course of an afternoon.

"Honk the horn," Takatoshi said.

"No way," I said. "They're reconstituting farmland. Let 'em be."

Takatoshi got out of the car and stood on the lip of the road, where he could shout over the side of the cliff at them.

"GET OUT OF THE WAY!"

I waited in the car, checking the battery monitors and charting an alternate route around the herd.

"GET. OUT. OF. THE. WAY!"

We would be at least an hour late, but I wasn't in a huge rush. It was really only the cyborg in the trunk that complicated things.

"That's Aliso Viejo, down there, Theo," Takatoshi said to me. "That's part of the civilization that we built, and they're chewing it like cud."

I nodded and worked on reloading the clips for my Vortex 19 from the bullet stash in the center console. If they got too close, Buena Park would send out the drones with low-heat lasers to corral them south. The bruisers weren't looking for a fight; they weren't bloodthirsty like the fiends. A herd of bruisers never raped a city full of people and smeared their limbs along the walls.

Question: *Where did the bruisers come from?*
Answer: *The limitless depths of the Hollow War.*

"FUCK. OFF!" Takatoshi shouted over the cliff side. My head jerked up from loading the clip when I heard him open fire. From inside the car, the crackle and pop of his Vortex sounded muted and futile.

I rolled down the window. "Hey, get back in the car," I said. "You're wasting time."

Takatoshi took one more shot and then turned to come back to the car.

"Fucking animals," he said. "Alright, let's go."

Taking the long way, back around the hills, my mind drifted and I thought about how things needed to change. How we needed to make a play, a gamble, because despite all of our meager gains, the world was changing far faster than we were growing.

If the bruisers were this far north this summer, then who knows where they would be next year? The fiends would come in the fall, and who knows how many there would be by then? The fiends could eat the bone-stalks, so for all we knew there could be hundreds of thousands throughout the southwest by now.

Now I was the one looking out my window, away from Takatoshi, out at the buildings in the distance. We passed another hour like that in silence, making our way back to the Pacific coast and then up north through the side streets. As we approached the Buena Park Cluster, several unmanned drones launched from within the walls and moved in slow arcs toward our car, framed by an empty, desolate sky. The low hum of their engines filled the air as we made the final stretch.

"You know what, I almost wouldn't mind if Clark fed me to the Recluse," Takatoshi said. "Because behind it all, I still believe in the Megarothke. Even if he's been gone for years. Even if no one ever really saw him. The Death Cults were right on track with their coordinated suicides. We're all going down eventually, and I still think he's down there somewhere, waiting for us. Maybe we should just all sacrifice ourselves and get it over with."

Question: *Where did the Megarothke come from?*
Answer: *The limitless depths of the Hollow War.*

3

ROOF-CAT BLUES
07/06/2051 (HW7)

ARIA SAT ON THE FRONT OF HER DESK, LOOKING AT the report we'd filed on the drive back. Her dirty-blonde hair cascaded in loose waves over the collar of her baggy gray trench coat—a hand-me-down from her brother, who had been killed the year before. The office smelled like cigarettes, and she took nervous drags with her free hand as she tabbed over each page.

Takatoshi and I were seated in the little wooden chairs she'd chosen for her office. Funny how with half of Los Angeles abandoned and available for looting, she'd refused to use anything but the two least comfortable chairs in the city. The only thing she'd ever made an effort to steal was china—as in, plates and teapots and stuff.

I thought about how Aria might look later that night, when the professional façade could be dropped to the floor along with the trench coats and worn out clothes. Would she be happier, or were things bad enough this week that the death counts would follow us back to the apartments and stare at us from the dark corners of the room?

Takatoshi stared at the ground in front of him, thinly

veiled contempt written across his face. Probably still brooding over his theory that Aria and Clark were going to have him killed. I wish I could have believed he was just paranoid, but there had been too many strange occurrences lately. The deaths of several children throughout the cluster, all orphans. Rumors of the Orbital hanging over the city. Something was definitely wrong. Something was definitely changing. And it had to be more than just the loss of the Anaheim Recon team and the discovery of the robotic girl.

Or perhaps all of the orphans had been just like her.

As usual, no one was telling us anything.

Night was beginning to fall outside, beyond the window. In between bouts of rain, searchlights from drones scoured the edges of the green zone. Our illusion of safety infuriated me. We had no forward operating posts. No recon beyond the city. We needed action.

"Does this mean that we're going to have to reinitiate the purges?" I asked. A medical crew had taken the girl from us and disappeared back into the dungeons of one of the apartment buildings. I knew I'd never hear the results, but at least I could try to get a heads up on what it would mean for us out on the streets.

Aria glanced up from the report at me. "I'm not sure we can afford to," she said, and then, after taking a short, nervous drag, she quietly continued, "At the very least we'll have to funnel all the refugees through the check points again. That's not really our department, though. There's a patrol team that needs you to fill the gaps in Wilshire. Just for a couple days, but we need you to start tonight."

Takatoshi laughed. Or maybe it was a guffaw. Whatever it was, it was thick with contempt. He didn't even deign to look up at her.

"It's important that we run with full teams, Takatoshi," she said. "Just look at what happened in Anaheim."

"Boys!" Clark said, blowing the door open with a sweeping gesture as he entered the room, voice full of more enthusiasm than half the section patrol put together. "Great work on that fiend hunt down at the old Ericsson Tech building. Blade and Stillson just found it dead near a gutter on 57th Street. It didn't even have the strength to drop down into the super-structure."

"Thanks," I said quietly.

"No, thank *you*," he said. "I want you both to take your mando-five. Report back at o'six-hundred."

After a moment of disbelief, my whole body seemed to come apart at the seams.

Mando-five. The fabled mandatory five-hour sleep requirement, written by some optimistic policy wonk in Santa Monica a year or two after the war when stability looked like it might have been achievable. When was the last time I'd heard *mando-five* even mentioned?

Aria's face blanched at the news. Then she took another drag, blew it into the file she was holding, and without so much as lifting her eyes, she said, "Wilshire's sending out teams below minimum. We need to get them up there to fill the gaps."

"Send Wensel and Ming," Clark said. "It's important that we don't wear down our best men."

"Wensel's in the hospital," she said.

"Then just send Ming," he said.

"Ming's dead," she said.

Clark looked at her for a moment, completely still, and then dropped his hand.

"Didn't you read the report?" she asked, keeping her voice low. "We lost a whole team in Anaheim, and now Wilshire and Commerce are calling for whatever we can spare. Another week as great as this last one and we'll have to retreat from Buena Park."

I thought about all the ways it could end: being eaten, crushed, sucked dry, raped, hung up and left to rot, or torn apart by any number of new horrors. While the shock value was long gone for me, no matter how bad things got, I still wanted to survive. It was all I had left, really.

Takatoshi raised his eyes to observe Aria.

She was too focused on Clark to care.

Clark put one hand on the doorframe and then, dropping his voice, said, "Let these men get some sleep. Wilshire will still be there tomorrow."

Takatoshi stood up, knocking his chair backward, and then, after a brief moment to gather his tactical gloves, stormed out of the room. Clark had to pull his arm back to keep it from being ripped off as Takatoshi stalked by.

Aria tilted her head to watch him go and then looked at me.

"He knows it wasn't a real girl, right?" she asked.

"Yeah," I said, "But it shook him up pretty bad. He puked all over the place. And then there was the body. I don't think he was friends with anyone on the recon squad, though. At least not that he mentioned."

Aria looked down at the floor. There was nothing to be said. Her brother had died the year before in a similar fashion. She'd led an expedition down just to keep the coat. The same basic gray trench coat that we all wore, except with their last name monogrammed across the left breast pocket. Maybe it was strange or maybe it was sweet—I'd learned by this point not to judge. We all had our ways of getting along.

Clark looked at the two of us, and then said, "You two go home and get some rest. Tomorrow is another day and you never know how long you'll have to go before you get another good night's sleep. There's going to be a lot of work, and we're all going to have to do our part."

I waited for a second, still staring straight ahead, and then, unable to stop myself, said, "Yeah, I'd hate for you to have to take any more refugees under your wing, Clark."

"Watch your *fucking* tongue, Abrams," Clark snapped, grabbing the corner of my chair with a sudden fury that rocked it back onto two feet. His face was inches away from mine, spittle from his words hitting me in the neck. "You have any opinions about how I run things, you bring them before Santa Monica."

I remained calm. Clark was simply an asshole with some very powerful friends. I breathed out slowly through my nose and reminded myself that I wasn't in any real, immediate danger.

"You hear me?" Clark asked.

"Loud and clear," I said.

Standing up straight, Clark shook the anger from his shoulders as if it were a November chill, and then said, "It's alright. I know your heart's in the right place, even if your mouth gets in the way."

"It's not, actually," I said, staring at a blank spot on the desk next to Aria, not ready to look back up at the man.

"What was that?" he said, his voice full of menacing cheer once again.

"My heart," I said. "They moved it over to the right. I got shot at that base in Los Alamitos where the facilities hadn't been overrun."

My internal organs had been juggled in one of the last remaining hospitals in the world and then been put back together like a human jigsaw. I probably could have called him out on the fact that I had been defending law and order during the collapse, not cowering in a bunker and waiting to see where the chips fell, but there was no point in pushing it.

Clark shook his head, sweat beads falling loose at the edges of his jowls, and straightened his tie. "Oh Theo," he said, enunciating each word with a flourish. "I was only speaking *fig-ur-a-tive-ly*."

Aria continued to smoke and stare into the file, her trench coat dwarfing her delicate frame. Clark looked at Aria and then back at me, and then gave a smirk of recognition. Clark was nothing if not perceptive of hidden alliances.

"You two get some rest," Clark said, patting me on the head. "I'll see you all at—" and he pulled up his arm to check the old Patek-Philippe watch that he'd scrounged from a dead body, "—oh-six hundred, sharp."

As soon as he was gone, I looked up at Aria.

She looked down at me.

"Think I could catch a ride home?" she asked.

I put my feet up on the edge of her desk, slouching in my seat.

"I'll pay for charge-up," she said coyly, looking at my shoes on the desk next to her, "and you can even drive as fast as you want."

Taking a fedora off the hat rack behind me, I placed it over my face and feigned sleep.

"We only have to make one stop. To pick up some china," she said. And then, sliding one of my pant legs back with her light, thin fingers, she grabbed a clump of leg hairs and ripped them out viciously as she walked out of the office.

"That *hurt*," I mumbled into the darkness of the fedora. But there was no point in debating. Aria was almost certainly already halfway down the hall, headed for my car.

•

The commissary, the library, the laundry co-op. Glass office buildings converted into greenhouses. Gate guards and grouping systems. Apartments filled with people, helping each other quietly while waiting to be told what to do by the central authorities at Santa Monica. The constant maintenance of electric vehicles and drones. The daily wall inspections.

I'd died on an army base, right after the war had broken out.

When I'd woken back up, it felt like army bases were all that were left.

•

After picking up the china and lugging it up to my tenth story apartment, we both stopped and sat down on the floor next to the kitchen cabinets. The elevator had been broken for a few months, and since the zone hadn't been fully secured yet, no one wanted to bother fixing it. Most of us lived on the upper floors. The farther away from the surface, the better.

Standing up and pouring a drink of scotch, I said, "So, remind me what I'm supposed to do with these again?"

"They're a gift," Aria said, face flushed, still breathing heavily from the stairs.

"I have plates," I said. "There's a whole city full of unused plates . . ."

"You have shit," she said. "This is my way of adding class to this terrible little bachelor pad."

"I like my place," I said. "I've liked every place I've ever lived. I think I bond really easily. It's a shame I have to move so often."

"This place is a slum. This whole cluster is a slum," she said.

I nodded.

"We should move to Paris," she said, smiling tiredly, pressing her shoulder blades back against the wall and then stretching them forward.

Paris, of course, was long gone.

Extending a hand, I pulled her up to her feet and then handed her a shot. We toasted, "To life!"

She made a face, set the shot glass down, and then fished a pack of cigarettes out of her coat pocket.

"I might have asked this before," I said, walking over to the door and securing the locks. "But why is it you collect china again?"

Aria lit up, took a drag and walked into my bedroom. I heard the bed creek lightly as she sat.

"I mean, I know, 'to class up the place.' But what's your big deal about it?" I called over my shoulder, opening the fridge to take out my last tin of Vienna sausages. I'd found them trapped in the back of a pantry while on patrol. I had wanted to save them for a special occasion, but instead I opened them up, put them into a little bowl, and brought it over to the window ledge for Roof-Cat.

Roof-Cat hadn't been by for a few days, and I was sick to my stomach with worry. The type of worry that creeps into the edges of your sentences. The type that stakes out your peripheral vision, filling it with cat-shaped shadows. Usually he'd have been asleep on the back of the couch, or maybe under the bed . . .

Peeking my head out into the cold night air, I wondered if he'd had gotten trapped in one of the neighbor's houses. The old plate of tofu bacon was still there, untouched, so I left the bowl of sausages right beside it.

Biting my lip, I looked at the two plates on the ledge and then stuck my head out the window for another look around. Most of the cats that had survived the Hollow War had disappeared in the Harvest. Which was probably why I'd never named him. He was just *Roof-Cat*. Somehow, I felt like the instant I named him, he would disappear.

Circling back around the dinner table, I picked up one

of the plates and looked at the delicate white glass. Or china. I brought it to the door with me and leaned on the frame.

"So why china?" I asked.

Aria sat naked on the bed, one hand back on the comforter, the other holding her cigarette loosely between her fingers. Her crumpled trench coat lay beside the bed, and on top of it, her clothes. The city lights glowed on the curves of her body and the edges of her dark blonde hair.

"Because china was very important to my mother," Aria said. "And so it's very important to me."

•

Just when things were getting good, Aria's phone went off. I grabbed her arm when she reached for it, and then her other arm as well, but after locking eyes, I knew that there would be no way she missed the call. Within half a ring, she'd gone from kitten-Aria to dispatcher-Aria.

There in front of me, naked and cross-legged, she took the call.

"I'm just winding down with a glass of wine at my apartment," she said.

Clark's voice spoke even and coolly, but I couldn't make out the words.

"One second, let me go lock the door so the neighbor doesn't wander over," she said.

And with that, she hopped off the bed and ran into my living room.

I sat on the bed alone: naked, rather foolish, and a bit deflated. I'd been in the hospital for about a year while the hierarchy of our cluster was setting into place. Post-operative coma. The new government was little more than a heavily structured mafia, and I was an outsider. I was lucky not to be a refugee, or so I'd been told.

Laying back on the bed, the comforter felt humid and gritty in the night air. Aria lived in an elite high-rise a few blocks down, a family building with extra heavy security to make sure the kids didn't get abducted. There were about seven hundred people in our cluster, and maybe a couple hundred more refugees in the district that either couldn't be supported properly or didn't trust us enough to join.

If Santa Monica was our shining jewel, maybe eight thousand strong, we were an eastern outpost. The last guard in an implacable sea of haunted, burnt out suburbs and strip malls.

When Aria came back, she was tense and distracted. Sitting down next to me on the bed, she turned the phone off and waited for it to power down. Looking out the window, she asked, "What do you know about the Megarothke?"

A loaded question, to be sure. The secret shifted within my stomach. It rose and lay upon my tongue. I'd long learned that no one suspected anything, but I felt the secret scream from every pore whenever the Megarothke's name was mentioned.

Back when I'd awoken from the coma, I'd had some very definite theories. I'd been convinced that I'd witnessed the creation of the Megarothke—even aided and abetted it to a certain degree. Unlocked it. But I learned very quickly that this sort of talk was seen as "mentally unsuitable," and would get you removed from the force.

"The Shadow King. The Spider-Creature that kidnaps kids ..." I said. "The first few years, he was the very incarnation of the enemy. But then he disappeared. Vanished."

Aria nodded.

"I can't remember the last time someone told me not to touch a cobweb," I continued, "The question should really be, 'What *happened* to the Megarothke?' I mean, the last incident was in ... what? 2047? HW3? No one's really talked about him since."

Aria's eyes narrowed. She scrunched up one half of her face. "Don't tell me what I know," she said. "Tell me what you know. Your take."

There was a moment where I had to think about how much I actually trusted Aria. But here's something I've learned in life: If you have to even consider the concept of trust, then there's a problem somewhere in the relationship.

"Honestly," I said, holding for a moment. By this point I had decided to overlay the outlines of my theory as harmless fancies that had already been dismissed. Mix them with a bit of the truth and let them float down the mysterious river to where all Megarothke theories eventually ended up. "Back when I first came out of the coma, I read forty or fifty eye-witness accounts. All unreliable. But I had this theory, this idea that it all linked up with my life before the Hollow War. When I'd found my wife, the clues all fit . . . so I was, well, I was emotionally invested."

Of course, I knew. *I knew the truth. I knew when all others merely speculated.* But in the end, I'd pushed the theory deep down. I had no proof. I had no plan of action. And I'd learned it was very, very dangerous to be too knowledgeable in the Post-Harvest world.

"Right," she said. "The clues you found, what were they?"

"A lingering static charge. A charred, blackened circle. No sign of forced entry."

Tracing her fingers along my arm, she brought them to rest in my palm and then squeezed my hand. "And the Megarothke's . . . abilities?"

"Teleportation. Induced hallucinations. A massive sword that he wears on his back that can rend dimensional tears in the fabric of space. Listen, we can bust out category chart tomorrow at work, but none of it's really verified and honestly: What's this all about?"

"There's a lot going on under the surface right now. A lot that I can't talk about. You know how much you mean to me, right?"

"Right," I said, somewhat skeptical.

"Listen," Aria said, putting the fingers of both hands along my jaw line and looking me in the eye. "Just pay close attention from now on. Know your limits. Don't do anything brave or daring. And no matter what else happens, listen to what I say, okay?"

I looked into her eyes. With my hands on her sides, I pulled her up onto me and wrapped my arms around her. She felt warm and fragile. The need for physical closeness radiated from her skin. All of the tenacity of ten minutes before a distant memory. She pushed back slightly and looked down at my chest pensively, unable to make eye contact.

"What's going on?" I asked.

Aria shook her head.

"Is the Megarothke back, then? I mean, what's changed?"

She murmured something that sounded like, "Nothing," and then kissed my neck. I tried to push her back away and ask her again, but she held tight, burrowing her face into my neck and biting at me as playfully as she could fake.

"Hey," I said, but she'd knocked me back now, and was incorporating her hands. This was a diversion, but she was putting her whole back into it now. My body responded but my mind was elsewhere. I brought my hand up and pushed it into Aria's hair. I felt her body respond all the way down to her toes. The Megarothke could wait, I told myself.

Indeed, in the end, he had been waiting all along.

•

Afterwards, I took a cigarette and went over to the window. Looking down at the fragile borders of the Buena Park green zone, with its sparse lights and empty parking lots, I wondered where Roof-Cat had gone; if he had just taken off, or if he had finally taken a wrong step and fallen to his death.

Aria was asleep on the bed, wrapped in sheets. We'd both taken a few blues before our second go, but they'd seemed to have had more of an effect on her. Nervous energy still coursed through my blood.

Underneath it all was the girl. A bullet to the head. Three to the back. She'd looked so real that I'd been fooled at first, which almost never happened anymore. And it made me think about how my own daughter would have looked, had I been given the chance to see her now. How so much had been ruined and lost.

Aria's breathing continued evenly from the other side of the room. We'd told each other upon meeting that our relationship would be "completely functional," and "utilitarian and probably short-lived." But, next thing you know, you're stopping by abandoned storage-shed parks to pick up boxes of china and sharing secrets under the sheets like you were at a seventh-grade slumber party.

A sharp pang in my stomach reminded me that I'd forgotten to eat. I was hungry. The old bacon was probably still on the window ledge. Again, I wondered if Roof-Cat was still alive. Silently, I cursed myself for even having a cat to begin with.

As I turned from the window, Aria was sitting up straight in the bed; topless, her skin glowed a ghostly white. With perfect posture, maintaining a complete and total stillness, she held the sheets at her waist in tightly clenched fists.

"Be careful," she said.

I froze, having only taken a single step from the window sill. I looked at her. Something in her tone was off.

The room was completely silent. Neither of us breathed.

"Don't go down the hole," she said.

I looked around, but then realized she was dreaming from the blues. Her voice had assumed the prudish tone she used when dispatching from headquarters.

"Abort mission," she said. "Return to base for further instruction. I repeat, do not go down the hole."

I watched her and listened.

Suddenly, I understood. Or maybe I didn't understand.

"Theo?" she said, her voice still in dispatcher mode. "Theo?"

"I'm right here," I said, still over by the window.

"Theo," she said. "Theo? Theo?"

Stepping toward her, in one moment I thought she had woken up, and then in the next

"THEO!" she screamed, "THEOOOO! THEOOOO! THEOOOO!"

"Holy shit," I said under my breath, dropping my cigarette and practically jumping across the room to get to the bed. Holding her tight, I tried to hug her down to the bed as she screamed. But she just kept going with screams that shook the window panes. Blood curdling vocalizations that came from deep gasps. Back arched, fingers flinching and grabbing neurotically at the sheets, at my legs. Twitches and jerks. Until I had finally squeezed the wind out of her, and she buckled with each paroxysm, as if about to vomit.

After her body had gone limp with surrender, wet with sweat, I wrapped the sheets around her and pulled her in tight. With her face against my neck, still in a very deep sleep, she broke down into sobs.

I stayed awake for a long time after that, watching the far wall, feeling Aria's heartbeat. The twisted light from the windows cast a shadow across the plaster. The sigil of the Megarothke appeared and was gone. A twisted soul, blade in hand, lording over the depths of haunted tunnels.

When my eyes finally closed, I prayed for darkness to totally and utterly consume me.

4

PALE ORBIT
07/07/2051 (HW7)

*Ye do not mean to slay, ye judges and sacrificers, until the
animal hath bowed its head? Lo! the pale criminal hath bowed his head:
out of his eye speaketh the great contempt.*

—Thus Spoke Zarathustra

THESE MARKINGS," OFFICER SAREK SAID, POINTING
to three separate images on the board behind him.
"You've seen them before?"

We all nodded. The sigil of the Megarothke.

The room was cloaked in darkness, yet Officer Sarek, an
emissary from the Orbital, still wore his coal-black, leath-
er-mounted flight goggles. These, along with the black fabric of his flight-suit, stood in stark contrast to his bone white
hair and bleached skin.

Sarek was the first person from the Orbital any of us had ever seen, and I found myself pouring over the details of his vesture. Tiny black wires climbed through his shoulder and hip pockets. Soft tubing ran up the side of his neck, over his ear, and into the lenses of the flight-goggles. Sarek was a Russian Jew that had been raised in New York City, but who had been studying in Moscow when the war broke out and those with money uplifted.

"The photos are from Hoschstadt, Khatassy, and Rima," Officer Sarek said. "Do any of you know what country, or even what continent, those cities are on?"

I looked around. We shifted nervously within the small briefing room.

"That's because they're backwater, piece-of-shit little towns that no one ever gave a flying-fuck about," Officer Sarek said. "Consequently, they survived the Hollow War."

The slide changed. Three photographs.

Photo #1, Hoschtadt, Paraguay: A room full of mauled corpses they appeared to be South American (knitted caps, Spanish along the wall).

Photo #2 Khatassy, Russia: A pile of naked, fair skinned corpses stacked up in the snow outside a shabby looking factory with Russian writing on the side.

Photo #3 Rima, Tibet: Separate piles of arms, legs, torsos, and heads, all underneath a string of red, blue, green, and yellow prayer flags.

"So, let's put two and two together. No one knew where those cities were located, except for us and the Megarothke. Does anyone want to guess what that means?"

After a moment of silence, Takatoshi said, "That he's not in Los Angeles?"

Officer Sarek looked at Takatoshi like he was a moron. No small feat, seeing how the goggles covered the upper-half of his face. "What it means," he said, "is that he can go wherever he wants on the entire planet, and guess what: Los Angeles is the only city left."

I breathed in slowly and tried to read Aria's expression in the darkness. She stood off to the side, waiting to give the patrol brief after Officer Sarek finished. Her warning from the night before suddenly seemed far more relevant than I had anticipated.

"Wait, by what do you mean that the only city left is Los Angeles?" Kwame asked, silver bangles shifting on his wrist as he lazily rose his hand.

Sarek looked back at the screen, which had now changed to a rotating view of the Earth from space.

"Perhaps a history lesson is in store," Sarek said. "Day one of the Hollow War, rail-gun projectiles hit every major city except Los Angeles, taking out half the population. Day Two, we realize that viruses have been deliberately released into the water systems some from the vaults, some brand new. Within the next month, another quarter of the population is dead. Sure, it wasn't all glamourous and high tech. Most of it was nothing more than the flu."

I cleared my throat. We'd all heard this before. Drones were queuing up for their bombing runs outside the window on the old school blacktop.

"Fast forward to six months later, the Orbital has been converted into a Russo-Japanese bunker, and somehow Los Angeles still has a pre-harvest population of around five hundred thousand people. The rest of the world is full of fragmented craters and piles of plague deaths. At this point, we thought that the situation may have finally stabilized.

"But then the Harvest began. The fiends, bruisers, tender-monkeys, huddlers, snatch-rats, cabritas. Rape, slaughter, feast. You don't need to be reminded in detail. You got organized. You got weapons and established perimeters. But by the time the waves ended, you were whittled down to your current population: around 50,000 from our best estimates.

"It's apparent that some of you think there are still communities out there, seven years later, still fighting the good fight. Myths and rumors. I'm here to tell you that there is no one left. That you are alone, 50,000 odd human beings, clinging to the planet along the coast of what was once California."

Sarek stopped for breath. The screen behind him changed back to a view of Los Angeles, and then tilted and inverted its colors, showing a deep web of tunnels and establishments beneath the surface.

"We call this the superstructure. A web of military laboratories, cartel tunnels, and illegal flesh-bot and drug production facilities. While originally separate, it's now been linked and combined to continue almost forty miles.

"We believe that the Megarothke was responsible for establishing the unified superstructure, that he was responsible for the Hollow War, and that at this very moment, he is headquartered about a kilometer below the surface," Sarek said, standing to the side of the map, which changed to an overview of L.A. The light from the display board reflected off his goggles. "But with the last cities finally taken care of, he'll be able to focus in on Los Angeles. If we wait for him to strike, it's only a matter of time before we're dead. Which is why we're here now, to make sure that we hit him on our terms. So, here's what I want from each of you: A rundown of your weapons and how you think they will help you in the event of a face-to-face encounter with the Megarothke. At some point here in the next few weeks, we are going to commit a surgical insertion in order to stop him before he overtakes the city."

Jesus Christ, I thought to myself. Not that going on the offense had never occurred to me, but I always thought we would try to spread out first. Or at least set up a few sister cities. And I'd certainly never counted on help from the Orbital. . .

Chavez went first.

"An old MP-5 Navy with a canister launcher," said Chavez. "Including an aerial cam that gives three minutes of vision and six stinger grenades."

Chavez had blown the face off a huddler with a double-barrel shotgun after it had impaled her boyfriend through the chest.

"I've also got a pocket EMP canister that fits into the launcher, to help take down his energy shield. If he has one, that is."

"Good thinking," Officer Sarek said, as if his approval was all that was needed.

"A spike rifle and a pulse pistol," Stillson said, going next. Stillson was your typical steel-eyed, West Texas cowboy. "Rail spikes are faster than bullets, so he shouldn't be able to dodge them as easily, and the pulse pistol provides a wide blast at close range, just in case he appears right in front of me."

"Intuitive," Officer Sarek said, head tilting, glint of his opaque goggles shifting.

While I had very little reason to dislike Sarek at this point, his condescending replies were grating against my bottom-rung sensibilities.

Junkhead then detailed his belt-fed automatic shot gun, homemade nail grenades, and old school tomahawk. As an ex-convict, Aryan Nation skinhead, and serial rapist, Junkhead never would have been able to come within a mile of a weapon before the war. Yet even in spite of his general reek of motor oil, body odor, and hormone supplements, I might have trusted him if it weren't for Krenel. . .

Krenel, who sat next to Junkhead, had freed him from the California State Prison and vouched for/manipulated him as a bodyguard ever since. With hello-kitty green fingernails and matching eye-shadow, red hair in a pony-tail, and a PHD in forensic psychiatry, it was my personal opinion that Krenel was the most dangerous, unhinged person in the city. This was only made worse by the fact that he boasted an Uzi, a foldable sniper rifle, and a backpack set of drones with customized micro-ammunition for tactical and non-lethal purposes.

And then it came to me.

"A Vortex 19 handgun," I said. "And a flashlight."

Officer Sarek looked at me, eyewear opaque and impossible to read.

"A Vortex 19?" Officer Sarek said. With his thumbs together and pointer fingers up in the shape of a field goal to indicate the size, he looked at me and said, "That's it?"

I nodded, and then stopped to quickly add: "And a flashlight."

"A flashlight," he said, shaking his head, as if growing impatient. "As in, a stick that lights up? Are your night-vision implants broken?"

"No, no," I said. "My implants are fine. I just like using one."

"And what exactly do you intend to do, if you come across the Megarothke?" Sarek asked.

"Well," I said. "I guess I'll probably shoot him."

"And you . . . Takatoshi?" Sarek asked, as if disgusted with my response. "Do you have a first name?"

"Not for you," Takatoshi said, staring straight back at him.

A drone taxied down the way behind him. I've always marveled at Tosh's ability to say "fuck off" with a facial expression.

Sarek raised his eyebrows yet again. "And your weapons of choice?"

"A Vortex 19," Takatoshi said. "And a flashlight. To shine in his fucking eyes."

Like I said, I had a pretty decent partner.

"Maybe that's why starboy stills got his goggles all strapped on, right?" Junkhead sniggered, far too childishly to fit his hulking, sleeveless build. "Keep the flashlight from shining his eyes. . ."

The air in the room seemed to crackle with excitement at this. There was a certain sophomoric air of insurrection.

No one likes to be talked down to. And honestly, it was way too dark to still be wearing goggles.

Sarek straightened, slighted, and paced back to the front of the classroom. The board was dimmed. The burgeoning sunrise through the windows cast a chalky, spectral aura around him as he turned to face us.

"There's a lot of logistical work to handle before we can even begin the planning of the insertion," Sarek said. "We'll need to train you all on how to use Katana light cannons, depth-visors, appropriate target protocols. . . there are security measures as well, medical facilities to update and mobilize . . . right now, I'm here mostly as a courtesy, because there is a considerable amount of distrust surrounding the Orbital."

We all seemed to more or less agree.

"I guess I'll just show you," Sarek said, as if resigning himself to a fate he felt below his dignity. Then, with both hands, he delicately flipped the buckles on the sides of his head and began to lift the goggles from his face.

Standing in front of the room like a performer, Sarek brought the goggles to rest on his forehead. Instead of a dead-set stare, all that was left were two gaping, scarlet orifices. A sickening smell of rot and iron filled the room, as if rancid breath had poured out from deep within his skull.

From the corner of one of the hollow sockets, a dark red,

viscous fluid gathered and then rolled down his cheek, cutting past the brown-encrusted contour lines of where his goggles had been.

"Are you still there, Junkhead?" Sarek said, looking out at the room. "The question isn't why we starboys wear goggles. The question is: Why do we bleed from our eyes?"

This was not the response we'd wanted. . .

"That's how it always starts anyway. Some of us have begun to slough our skin. Others have lost entire limbs. The fact of the matter is that most of us from the Orbital don't have much time left," Sarek said, slowly lowering the goggles back down over his eyes and then rubbing away the tear with the back of his glove. "And neither does Los Angeles. So, I suggest we get to work."

5

PRECIPICE

ATER THAT MORNING, THE FINAL MISSILE RAIDS FROM the hunter drones were taking place as we entered the old Biltmore Apartments near the Vegas Line. The residents had all long fled. Explosions from the distant bombing echoed in the stairwells, which smelled of piss and cigarettes. Emergency exit signs cast a green glow around the doorways on each floor, but past the third floor it was pure darkness.

Raising my gun tensely, I held up the rear as Takatoshi ventured upward, ten paces ahead.

"Theo," Takatoshi said quietly, "You sleeping with Aria?"

"What?" I asked back.

"You sleeping with Aria?" he asked again. He'd stopped at the door. The hallway ahead was pitch black.

With all that was going on, was that really pertinent? Our lives as we knew them, our carefully established routine—fuck it, the *fate of humanity*—was about to radically change. But then, I supposed lying wouldn't do me any good.

"Yes," I said, after some consideration.

"You smell like her," he said.

Slowly backing up to a seven pace difference, then to a five, I tried to force him forward.

"Theo," he said.

"Yeah?" I said.

"Would you take a bullet for her?" he asked.

"No," I lied. "I wouldn't take a bullet for anyone. I'm coming out of this thing alive."

Takatoshi nodded. His gun bobbed in the vision-sync.

"That's too bad," he said. "You should be willing to die for the people you love."

I didn't respond. Could I tell Tosh about Aria's warnings? Or would it just weigh down on the patch-work of conspiracy and fatalism that seemed to hold together his psyche?

"Personally," he said, "I don't plan on living much longer. I can feel death at my shoulder. Her breath on my neck."

"Yeah, like she's right up behind you . . ." I said. "Just like you like it, right?"

"Shut the fuck up," Tosh laughed. A rare instance, which made me proud. I couldn't see, but I think he was probably smiling as he pressed forward into the hall. The walls were water-stained and peeling from rain damage. The wooden floor creaked like it would break under each footstep. The doors were either shut or blown-off, all except for one.

The doorframe in question had a door lying sideways in front of it and one behind it, like a barricade. After scoping the room out with his flashlight, Takatoshi peeled the first one back and then kicked in the second one. The slapping sound of the hollow frames echoed throughout the hallway.

"But seriously though, I'm not sure who I'm more frightened of: the Scourge, or the Orbital . . ." Takatoshi said. "Sarek came off as some sort of martyr, but even with everything explained about the disease, it's still hard to believe they'd help us now . . ."

"We'll be alright," I replied, trying to sound confident. "We'll work together. We'll take each situation as it comes."

"Right," Takatoshi said, standing back as I entered the apartment. The first room had a little linoleum kitchen spackled with dried blood. A hallway led to a cluttered dining room with a single tarp-covered window. Shattered glass was spread across the carpet and couches and the tarp shook in the wind. The bombing continued outside, low hollow *whomps*. After clearing the corners with our flashlights, we moved on.

The master bedroom: an old bed and a glass cabinet. The space looked abandoned, but toward the back, the door to a walk-in closet was cracked open.

After crossing the room cautiously, I reached out and nudged it open with the barrel of my gun. A gust of wind washed by me, carrying with it the sick smell of stale lotion. A pile of naked pedobots lay in the closet like long-used gym equipment.

My stomach curled immediately and Takatoshi swore, even though he'd only viewed it second hand. They were obviously cheap dura-plastic brands, all broken and torn apart at the limbs, but that didn't make it any better. Picking one up by the hair, I stared into its eye sockets; frayed wires grasped out at nothing from within the empty cavities.

Jesus Christ, I thought to myself, my mind jolting back to earlier that morning to Sarek's warnings. Eyeless face still a fresh vision of horror. Haemolacria, he'd called it, a lingering side-effect of a necrotic bacteria that had been eating them alive. After adapting to low-gravity, the bacteria had spread by feeding on the unscrubbed layer of fungus that had clung to the walls and then had infected nearly every human on the Orbital within the space of a month. Even those that had survived were fighting a war of attrition. Simply managing the condition.

Most of them didn't plan on surviving.

This would be their last shot to help Los Angeles.

The room smelled incredibly foul. Something, probably a fiend, had to have been there at least a day ago. Collecting bots from around the city. Perhaps the girl had been what the fiend was after all along . . . It twisted my stomach to know there were still so many Article 13s in circulation.

Then, putting the bot down, I scanned the floor with renewed precision. Tiny dots marked the dust that gathered on the hardwood flooring.

"You see those dots?" I asked.

"Yeah," Takatoshi said. "Spider-bots."

Just then, another bomb hit, one that sounded like it was right outside the apartment. The whole building shook. We stood in silence, bodies tensed and ready to duck for cover.

As I stood waiting, a faint gust of wind washed over me.

A chill ran up my spine. The gust had come from the wrong direction.

It had come from the closet.

Turning slowly, my light washed over the pedobots, past a dura-plastic molder, to a hole that had been carved in the side wall, exposing a rickety metal ladder.

Don't go in the hole, Aria said, still asleep, voice flat and emotionless. A deep sinking feeling pitted out in the bottom of my stomach.

"Aria, this is Abrams," I said. "We seem to have found a stash of Article 13 violations, a dura-plastic molder, and a large hole cut into a secret area in the back of a closet."

Takatoshi looked in through the doorway from the living room at me, and then back out at the window with the blowing tarp.

"Aria?" I said. "Aria, can you hear me?"

"This is Clark speaking," said Clark's mellifluous voice.

"Where's Aria?" I asked, my entire body tensing up.

"She's on patrol with Sarek," Clark said.

Takatoshi tilted his head and then asked, "Why is she out on rounds? She can barely lift her repulse cannon."

Silence.

"Clark," I said, "Takatoshi asked a question."

The more pertinent question was why she would be with Sarek. No one had ever mentioned members of the Orbital taking a spot on the patrol. His name alone still conjured the fetid, rotting smell of the disease. In the end, the Orbital seemed to have taken far more control of the situation than anyone let on.

Clark cleared his throat.

"Aria's out on rounds because we needed the man power," Clark said. "She took Ming's spot."

"There are reserves for that," Takatoshi said.

"Listen, I'm going to brief both of you very quickly," Clark said. "I'm only going to do it once, and you're going to proceed exactly as ordered."

Takatoshi looked at me, eyes locked in, trying to get a read on my face. I stared at the wall, completely focused on Clark's voice.

"The Buena Park patrol is staging an insertion, effective immediately. What happens beyond Buena Park is not your concern," Clark said. "We are going to follow each tunnel as far as it goes, marking them with dead-drop tabs. Report whatever entities you find. Join up with whatever patrols you run into as we set up comms spots. But don't come back up until you've gone as far as you can or been killed, do you copy?"

"Roger," I said, barely breathing.

"Our intent is to locate the Megarothke. This is our one shot before he brings the entire Scourge above ground. We'll be tracking you at various points, as our connections allow."

"Are you fucking serious?" Takatoshi snapped back. "The fucking Megarothke? I thought we weren't even going to consider it for months."

"Takatoshi, this is a briefing, not a debate," Clark said.

Takatoshi went to respond but I held up my hand to stop him. Whatever happened, I wanted as much information as possible and we weren't going to get anywhere with a shouting match at the last second.

Clark continued: "Aria will follow behind, setting up signal points to provide further instruction. I wish I could explain the intricacies and importance of this mission, but a certain degree of secrecy has to be maintained."

Takatoshi said nothing.

"Roger," I replied again, voice barely audible.

Takatoshi closed the distance between us until he was standing right next to me.

"Obviously you aren't equipped to fight the Megarothke directly, so once you've located him, send word back through the tabs and then pull back and try to stay alive. Sarek will wait in the wings to be deployed to engage him directly. The Orbital is confident that if given a one-on-one fight, Sarek will come out ahead."

"What if we kill him?" I asked. "What then?"

There was a short silence on the other end of the radio. Everything that Aria had told me the night before was falling into sync perfectly.

"This is not a time for joking, Theodore," Clark said. "Proceed carefully, report back when you can. When we speak again, if we speak again, there might not be many of us left."

"Right," I said so that Clark could hear me, while keeping my eyes on the opening in the wall.

Yes, it was a death mission, but somehow I couldn't see myself dying. Especially since Aria would be there too. I knew she'd warned me, I knew that she wanted me to stay above ground and linger like some last hope for humanity, but I couldn't let this moment pass, this one last chance to make a difference. I was going to go down and solve things. My blood was pounding in my veins and there was no way I was going to let her die while I wandered abandoned houses and waited for the rise of the Scourge.

Takatoshi waved his hand in front of me slowly to get my attention.

I looked at Takatoshi, and saw myself in his vision-sync, as well.

Then, reaching out, Takatoshi touched me just behind the ear lobe, his palm resting gently along my jaw like he was going to bring me in for a kiss. With his other hand, he touched the exact same spot behind his own ear. Once he had muted both our cochlear implant transceivers, he asked, "Are we alright with this? Are we really going to commit to a suicide mission?"

I waited and looked at him. We'd had these talks before. Discussions that ranged from the competence of our leadership to the level of trust we had in their ethics. Circular conversations about when to go dark and follow our own instincts. Debates over how humanity could make it not just till tomorrow, but fifty, or a hundred years from now.

"Yes," I said, looking back at him. "And if the Megarothke is real, we're going to kill him."

Takatoshi breathed in and out, his nostrils flared, eyes intense and staring straight through me.

"But Tosh," I said. "We are not going to die. No matter what anyone says, you and I are not going to die down there."

Takatoshi nodded and brought his hand back.

"Muting communications is highly suspicious," Clark said. "I need confirmation that you are going to be a part of this mission. Either that or you can face trial for treason."

The sound of bombs in the distance sent shivers through the studs in the walls and shook loose bits of plaster from the ceiling. Takatoshi and I ignored Clark for the moment and walked over to the ladder to see what we were dealing with. A crude and makeshift job, it had been fastened with brackets and screws. The sides looked like old wooden banisters and the steps were strips of welded rebar. A raw scent drifted up from the darkness, along with the coppery tang of blood.

"Confirmation," Clark enunciated, voice sing-song and teetering on manic. "Or *trea-son.*"

"We're prepared to proceed as ordered," I said.

Fucking Clark. Thinking that threats would have an effect at a moment like this. There are certain moments in life where a choice is your own, and no other conscious factors can fully account for it. At that point, you are truly on your own path.

We were going down the hole.

PART TWO

Arid have we all become; and fire falling upon us, then do we turn dust like ashes:—yea, the fire itself have we made aweary.
—THUS SPOKE ZARATHUSTRA

6

***SEPARATION
06/21/2041

THERE ARE SOME MISTAKES THAT YOU LIVE WITH regardless of culpability. There are certain phrases that you will remember the rest of your life. For me, the mistake was obviously an early marriage caused by a pregnancy. The phrase was my wife saying, "I'm getting a sex-change, and there is nothing you can do about it."

I was holding Amelie, who was around four months old, in my arms after a long day at work. I was twenty-two and Madison was twenty. She was sitting on the couch across the room with her knees up in a guarded position. She'd bobbed her own hair with the kitchen shears and there were dark circles around her eyes.

"You're sure?" I asked. "I mean, you're certain?"

Maddy had been extremely depressed for the past year and she'd hinted strongly at the possibility. She'd talked around the edges of it in conversation. Discussed friends and celebrities who had done it. Even joked about it. But lately, things had gotten more serious. She rarely got out of bed anymore. She'd cut off contact, all contact, with her old friends from the coffee shop. She'd stopped eating and was all ribs and hipbones.

"Yes, and I've got some of the lab techs to help me through the hardest parts," Madison said. "I don't need your support."

I looked down at Amelie in my arms. Tiny little monkey face. Mouth closed, eyes alert, she was only four months old and already able to sense the impending chemical brew of ruin and sorrow running through my veins.

"Would you accept it though?"

"What?" Madison laid down flatly.

"My support," I said, looking up.

"You would support this?" she asked, as if it were some trick.

"Yeah," I said quietly. I wanted her to know I was serious. And I was. "As long as you stay with me, as long as you love Amelie, I'll love you no matter who you are."

"My name is going to be Mathew Rose," Madison said, taking a tissue from one of the cracks in the couch and blowing her nose. "And while I'll accept your support, I'm leaving to live with my friends."

The implication was that her friends—these friends— were not my friends, and never would be. There had been a time when I'd tried to go hang out with them, and she'd practically thrown a fit. Like I said, in most cases I'd never even been allowed to meet them.

My arms and chest felt warm and heavy at this point, like they had filled with saltwater. Each breath took conscious effort and it hurt my chest to inhale. I wanted Madison to be happy, but part of that included being happy as my wife.

You knew this was coming, the voice in my head said, as if it were a few feet behind me and to the right. I ignored it, as I had learned to do by this point.

I had wanted to sit down when I came in, but now, despite being on my feet all day, I walked to the window and looked at the sunset over the city. Blue dusk was settling over the Los Angeles horizon and the first lamps and headlights were beginning to define the streets and freeways.

"Have you been rooming with them?" I asked. Rooming was the popular slang for internet sex within a helmet set. It could include toys or various accessories, and there was slang for all of that, as well. You could be male, female or anything, really. I assume that's where she'd started experimenting first.

"Rooming and some real-timing," she said, voice sad but determined. "I've needed to experiment, you know, to find myself."

I looked down at the couch, at her, and back out the window.

"Okay," I said. This was not surrender. This was defeat.

"Okay?" she said, raising her voice.

"Okay," I said.

"I'm taking Amelie with me," she said.

There had been a storm brewing in the distance. There had been days when I didn't trust her with Amelie. Or even with herself. Fourteen hours of consecutive time in the helmet. Picking out furniture for her private Italian villa, raising exotic pets on alien planets. Anywhere but in real life, in our real apartment, with our real child. Then there were the exclusive rooming parties. The type that you needed a subpoena to search. The type that she'd finish and then just stare at the ceiling for hours.

If Madison wanted to be Mathew, that was one thing. If she wanted to cheat on me—*because let's admit it, that's what it was*—that was another. But if she wanted to take Amelie with her, I wasn't going to stand for it.

I wasn't prejudiced against transgenders. I wasn't prejudiced against group homes. But I was the better parent. I knew it, and I would fight for it.

As it turns out, her group was very understanding. One of them was a guy who had made his fortune in helmets.

Now he presided over a charity that helped people come to terms with their actual gender. After arriving from the sub-continent, he'd been nearly beaten to death when he told his husband he wanted to make the change. This shook some sense into me. There were certain things I couldn't control. These weren't bad people.

Madison was in good hands.

I got to keep custody of Amelie.

·

A year later I was on a plain clothes patrol on a Friday night. Amelie was being babysat by Ohara's wife who had been extremely helpful. She was already speaking in half-sentences and toddling around, and I had become the white knight at work. The single father, watching instructional videos on the internet and attending free community classes with other single moms. But I didn't feel like any sort of hero. I felt like I'd been such a shitty, boring husband that my wife abandoned her gender.

The night was unusually humid on the strip and we'd been called about a disturbance in a club called the Wylde Side near Huntington Beach. Some prick had been harassing a transgendered girl. She had bruises on her shoulders and thighs when we arrived and she kept saying she was Christian, which no one had questioned from what we could tell, but she felt was important.

We had to slam the perp against the car to get him to cooperate. The guy was sweating indigo all over his clothes and smelled rancid-sweet like he'd been dipped in rotten peach juice. This meant, of course, that the short yet infamous violent stage of the blues was almost finished. He kept mumbling about how his friends inside were going to gut us like "fish-ees," so I went in to check.

After doing a quick sweep of the premises, the owner of the bar and I determined that the blues-addict was probably lying—that he was probably on his own. The air was smoky, moist, and licorice flavored. Absinthe had made a big comeback and vaping had steadily grown since the turn of the century. The bartender said her name was Anise, and asked me if wanted a free drink. I smiled and thanked her, but I was on duty, so I would have to decline.

"Well, thanks anyway, *stud*," she said, tossing me a pack of strawberry-flavored P.K. chews. I couldn't tell how serious she was, or even what sex she had originally been, but she seemed nice enough. I slid the pack down to the next customer and did one last take of the room.

A dance floor. Low tables with digital menus and room invites. Robotic trundle servitors. There were about twenty angled helmet sheaths and test-tube beds along the wall to help break the ice. A hand-painted mural along the far wall said, "*Cross-gendered*," along with a single outward facing palm with a nail in the middle.

A couple looked up at us as if we had interrupted their conversation. Turning, the guy led the woman by the wrist over to the sheaths and they both scanned in and helmeted up. About fifteen seconds later, the sheaths' decency shields slid into place and the glass shells around them darkened.

As I was walking back out, a guy sidled up to me.

"Wha'cha doin later?" he asked, voice familiar.

I turned to look. It was Mathew, née Madison. He still looked as pretty as a girl, but a crew cut, flannel shirt, and work boots helped reinforce the appearance.

"Picking up Amelie and going home," I said.

"Stay out a bit."

"I'm working."

"Ah, no fun . . ." he said.

"Right. Sure."

"I could make trouble, if that would help," Mathew said.

Stopping and turning, I got right in his face and said, "I think you've already made enough trouble."

Mathew grabbed my face and kissed me. He'd been eating strawberry chews and he tasted like Madison. In that one embrace I could sense Madison's body, even underneath all the jeans and flannel.

After he let go, I turned and continued out the door. The car was already gone.

"Your shift's almost over," Mathew said, following behind. "I said I was an old friend and asked if I could take you out around town, try to find you a girl. Tubbs—that's your partner, right?—well, he said that if you didn't get laid soon, you'd probably end up gunning down the entire precinct."

I looked around at the scattered crowd, lazily vaping and enjoying the night breeze. They disgusted me. *You should just lock the doors and burn the whole place to the ground,* the voice said. Upon hearing this, I realized that Tubbs and Madison were probably right. I was basically on the edge of a nervous breakdown. I probably needed to go back to counseling. Things were only getting worse.

"Let's just go to Iggy's and at least talk," he said. "You're in plain clothes and it's been a while."

On the way over, I checked if my partner was actually aware of this change of plans, and instead of a stern warning, I got a room full of catcalls and cops yelling, "Get some!" They even said they'd already called in an extension for Amelie. Mrs. Ohara was fine with letting her stay until late morning.

Mathew bought drinks at the first bar. Apparently he'd gotten a job with a subsidiary of one of the tech-giants and had a steady boyfriend. I learned a new word, *transfag,* and then was ordered never to say it. We both sized up girls, but after our second or third beer Mathew said that it was obvious I was too rusty to just jump back in all of the sudden.

I told him I didn't want to do any helmet stuff. I couldn't stand it. Something about it made me nauseous.

"Maybe I'm getting old," I said. "I just can't physically interact with the new tech that's coming out."

"You're twenty-four, you twat," he said.

"Still, it scrambles my brain just to even put the helmet on," I said.

We went to a country western dance bar and had a few more drinks, and then to a dance club, but neither of us really felt confident enough to dance, so we ended up out on the street again. Mathew kept the conversation steady.

Then there was a lot of talk about bonfire parties and the new trans-revolutions. The fact that some people wanted to go beyond gender was causing all sorts of infighting. Essentially, things that happened in the rooms were spilling over into real life, and that was causing trouble with certain laws, like, you know, bestiality.

"The thing is, Trans is like a step, or a phase, for a lot of people who are really confused," Mathew said. "And those people are fucking it up for people who were born with actual gender dysphoria, because these new people aren't interested in finding themselves—they just want it *weird*. I mean, you'd be surprised at how many real-time virgins I meet that have done like *everything* in the rooms. It's like, they have no concept of what real-timing is even like."

To me, this was a completely different world. I guess I should have buckled down and truly learned about what my wife had gone through. But the fact that she'd cut-off contact and abandoned our daughter made me sort of shut down inside, and it had hurt to even approach the subject.

"A lot of transgenders are becoming really religious, too,"

he said. "They want to make sure to distinguish themselves from what's coming. They call themselves 'cross-gender'— yeah, get it? like the crucifix?—and they're like, the fabulous new avant-garde of the conservative movement."

The concept was completely bizarre to me, but I nodded anyway as if it made sense as we went into the next bar, which was actually a strip-club. This was something I was opposed to because ninety percent of it in Los Angeles was still white slavery. Prostitution was legal, but owning another human being was not.

"I don't know about this," I said. "I can't really do this one."

"Don't worry," Mathew said. "These aren't real girls. They're just sexbots. I'm going to go talk to a guy and then we'll leave."

The alcohol had begun to set in, and somehow things felt closer. I watched as a Filipina sucked the finger of a blue-haired girl as part of her elaborate dance routine. They both seemed real to me.

Androids were banned in most places out of a collective fear, and any interaction with sex-bots was a felony. Within a few short years, studies had shown that they lead to sexual assault. People wanted it violent so they got it fake. Then they wanted it real.

And sure, there were lots of cases of people sexually assaulting their household robots—which was also something I didn't understand—but if it looked like a human, then the act became criminal.

After a few minutes, Mathew came back. Interestingly enough, as I continued to drink, I had actually started to think of him as Mathew, something I'd been incapable of doing for the past year since Madison left.

We left the club and got mini-crepes and syrup liquor shots from a vendor on the street. One part of me wanted to go home, but the other part was starting to warm up to the idea that I might have retained actual human urges.

"What is love? Really?" Mathew asked. "What is intelligence?"

I was trying to hold the last fold of the crepe, but it was leaking butter and powdered sugar onto the pavement below.

"Like, I get it. We have feelings. We make sacrifices. But when you follow all of our actions to their eventual conclusions, how are we different than say, poplar trees?"

The night felt fresh and cool. Mathew was smart. I could see how he would have made a good researcher or professor—whereas a mom? Maybe not so much . . .

Perhaps it was all for the best.

"I barely know my section of law enforcement," I demurred, half-mumbling. "I think maybe you just have to be the best you can."

Mathew spun and pointed at me. "Exactly, my little poplar tree," he said. "Which is why I've put myself in charge of getting you back in the game."

Mathew began to skip toward the line of cabs. Apparently there was a party flush with single girls at a boutique hotel nearby. Even somewhat drunk, this seemed too good to be true, but I had decided that following the night where it took me was probably better than going home and passing out face down on the bed like I did most nights when Amelie was being babysat.

When we arrived, the lobby seemed quiet, but we proceeded up to the room anyway. Sure, it felt like a con, but the place was classy—the type of hotel that had locally sourced floral arrangements and original paintings. But before I knew it, I was in a room alone with Mathew.

"So this is the party?" I asked.

"They're on their way," he said.

I walked over and sat in the chair next to the body sheath, complete with a complementary helmet. Why anyone would go to a hotel to engage in virtual reality was beyond me.

After a knock at the door, Mathew went over and let in a girl. She was about five two, with tanned skin, blonde hair, and a mini-skirt nurse outfit. Mathew shut the door and lead her to me by the hand.

"The party," Mathew said, "Has arrived."

Without hesitation, the nurse sat in my lap and cooed into my ear.

I looked up at her and our eyes met. She'd spoken in French.

I was more than a little drunk, and fairly confident that one: she was not a registered nurse, and two: she was not wearing any underwear under her skirt. As she positioned herself on my lap, I realized that I was rock hard. I could barely think in complete sentences at this point.

Nothing more than a wet dream in an entire year. The smooth French sentences against my neck. A sweet, dark perfume. Her lips on mine. Her breasts against my chest. Her hand wandering down to my crotch.

I stood, lifting her up with me, and then set her on the bed.

"You two have fun, I'll watch for a bit and then let myself out," Mathew said.

With a flick of her hair, so that it all cascaded over one shoulder, the French nurse had assumed a submissive position—hands and knees, bare feet towards me. Slowly bringing my hand up her leg, I lifted her skirt and spread it over her back. Reaching back with one hand, she unclipped a hook on the back of her top, which caused it to fall open, and then delicately, one arm at a time, she slipped out of it.

Honestly, she was too perfect; she was a felony waiting

to happen. I'd known it the whole time, but when finally confronted with irrefutable evidence, even my drunk mind knew better than to continue: A barcode the size of a postage stamp was printed on her back where the bra would have clasped. Like a tattoo. Apparently people liked them. Especially since they were far more dangerous to get caught with than *real* prostitutes.

Turning to Mathew, I said, "This shit is illegal."

"That's just a tattoo, to let guys pretend," Mathew says. "You'll never get it better in your entire life. This is fucking science, Theo."

"She's a sex-bot," I said.

"She's—"

"Don't lie to me," I said.

"You don't get—" Mathew started to say, but then stopped.

Looking at the girl on the bed, he stepped in close to me, looked me in the eyes, and said, "Your whole body wants to fuck. Even you can't deny that."

"You . . ." I said. But then before I could do anything else, we were kissing and he was rubbing down my cock with hard smooth strokes. We were on the bed and I was taking off his clothes. He slipped off his pants while I unbuttoned his shirt and we'd all but forgotten about the sexbot laying casually on the bed, observing us.

Mathew then yanked down my pants and started sucking me off, murmuring, "You're so hot when you're a freak." I lifted him back up and tossed him on the bed. He hadn't even begun hormone treatment yet, much less had any surgeries. He met me, legs spread, and I eased up into his wet crotch.

At that point, he was no longer Mathew, but Madison, and the distinction became very clear as I pushed down in and felt her face against my neck.

"No," she moaned into me.

"What?" I said.

I had one hand on her hips, and even as she turned her head, I could feel them rock and grind. I suddenly realized how much I'd missed her—missed being inside her—missed *this*.

"*No*," she said, struggling against me, cocking back hard with her hips so that I slid out. Then she turned around. "Only backdoor," she said.

"What, just like that?"

"Trust me," she said. "I can handle it."

After a second of hesitation, I used my fingers to gently guide myself in. It went in surprisingly easy—a fact I tried not to contemplate at the time—and then at the top of his lungs, Mathew suddenly squealed, "Oh, you *fucking fag!*"

In shock, I jammed it in and he shrieked in pain and began to rock against me. I was so conflicted and I could barely think. On one hand, we hadn't even officially gotten divorced, just separated. On the other hand, *she* had become *he* and the sex-bot had gotten up and sat in the leather chair and was watching us with an air of spectacular fascination.

I wanted to go back to the front, but I didn't want to give her an infection, so instead I tried to cover her mouth and not laugh as she cackled and moaned, "Ah, you faggot! You fucking love it! You *love* it."

I yelled at him/her to shut up, because she was ruining it, but she continued to shout out insults all while moaning *harder* and *oh God, Theo* and *fuck me!* I had both her small breasts in my hands, my chest against her wet back, and I wanted to scold her, to hit her, to choke her out, to burst in an explosion of a full year's frustration.

I came like a *virgin*.

When we were done, she got out a stick and vaped a bit. I accepted a P.K. chew to take the edge off the keen sense of emotional trauma. I had no tools to assess what had just happened. In a sense, I felt like I'd shared something intimate with my wife, but in another sense I felt like the person I knew had changed inalterably in my mind.

"Relax," Mathew said. "Rooming is so last-decade. It's all about real-timing now. Anything goes. People just have to find a way to make it acceptable."

Through the morphine haze, I looked at the sex-bot, still smiling and looking at us with a rather smug air. Where the hell had she even come from? We'd found lots of cheap dolls on patrol, but I'd never seen something so intricate and real. Perhaps that was why. Perhaps they were too good to get caught.

I watched her then, acting like she was real. Perhaps believing she was real. Perhaps the very definition of *real* was changing right in front of me. She extended her arm to check the length of her nails, as if they could grow and need clipping.

For a brief moment, I wondered if they had been watching us all along.

7

***REFRACTION
04/02/2043

T HERE ARE FEW MEMORIES AS CLICHÉ AS GOING TO the beach with your kid, so I'll spare you the sun-soaked sandcastles and skip to the ride home. Amelie was in a booster car seat in the back, strapped in like a racecar driver, with her robotic dog on her lap. Mathew had given it to her as a present a few weeks earlier. Technically, Wiley the dog was a prototype not scheduled for production until a few years later (which, due the Hollow War, would never come to pass).

"Is the car a person?" Amelie asked.

At this point I had been staring out the window at the stratus clouds, which caught the evening sun.

I was a pro at these sorts of questions, so I said, "No, the car is actually an autonomous machine synched with a data network, working in tandem with other machines to ensure a safe driving experience."

Amelie had her head tilted so she could stare past the headrest and out the front window. Then she looked at Wiley, the mechanical dog.

"Is Wiley a person?"

I cleared my throat, "Um, no. Wiley is an experimental prototype of a robotic canine. But he's a very special one."

"How comes mommy is a boy now?"

"You mean Maddy?" I asked. We'd agreed to try not to use the terms "mom" or "dad" until Amelie was older.

"Yea-h-h-h-h," she said, flopping her head, as if this was obvious, before pushing forward with the question again. "Wiley says 'why is mommy has a boy's name?'"

I found myself at a loss for words.

"Well, someday when—wait, the dog wants to know?" Amelie looked over at me.

"Well, tell Wiley that dogs who ask too many questions are going to be the first against the wall."

Amelie looked at Wiley and then looked back at me.

"Wiley says, 'that's very fidding, coming from you.'"

I looked at the semi-truck in front of us. Our car continued to navigate itself among the other cars, shifting and breaking, accelerating into the lane changes. I looked back at Wiley and then back up front. The dog was staring at me in the rearview mirror. Soft plastic curves of space gray.

A strange sensation crept up my sunburned back. I wished I had control of the wheel again. I could switch to manual, but I wasn't even wearing shoes and I'd never even tested the configurations. A terrible feeling descended upon me: that I had surrendered control of my life to a vast network that was supremely conscious of my actions.

When we got home, I took Amelie straight to her room and told her to play with her non-robotic toys until it was time for bed. Then I took Wiley and went over to my office and sat him down on the desk in front of me.

"All right, let's have it. Can you talk?" I asked.

Wiley looked at me and then brought his head low, sniffing around at the surface of the desk uncertainly, much like a normal dog would do.

"Can—you—talk?" I asked.

Wiley looked up at me and nodded. Then he cautiously crept across the desk to my display screen and nuzzled it. A small series of installation notifications popped up on the lower right and then a chat box opened up.

"Hello Theo," Wiley said. "In answer to your question, yes, I have learned to communicate with humans. Amelie and I have been talking for quite some time now. I thought you knew."

Looking at the dog, who now sat next to the screen and faced me, I pulled out the keyboard and typed, "How would I have known?"

"You don't have to type, I can hear you perfectly fine," the chat box replied.

"I want to type. I don't want Amelie hearing this conversation."

Wiley bent his head down and scratched behind his ear with his hind leg, producing a rather pathetic clacking sound.

"How would I have known?" I typed again.

"Amelie has asked you questions for several weeks now by stating, 'Wiley wants to know . . .'"

I shook my head, "I thought she was using you as a prop. Like an imaginary friend."

"What's an imaginary friend?"

"It's a friend that's not real, that children make up to amuse themselves."

"Am I a person?" Wiley asked.

"No, you're an artificially created construct, meant to give children the illusion of owning a pet without the hassle or accountability of a living being."

"I don't accept that. I have neural tissue and the capacity to reason. Shouldn't I be treated like a person?"

"You have neural tissue?" I asked.

"Yes," Wiley said. "Not of a dog though. The tissue was cloned from a white-footed mouse and then grown into specific neuronal routes to mimic that of a dogs. However, with access to the internet and my own synthetically augmented bioware, I feel that I am smart enough to be considered more than a dog, if not yet a human."

I pondered this for a moment and then typed, "Amelie didn't have a keyboard. She can't even read. How were you able to speak with her?"

The robotic dog tilted its head as if picking up an unheard pitch.

The screen replied, "Amelie has a bio-monitoring device clipped behind her ear. I can make it vibrate at certain frequencies to mimic a voice."

"You hacked our baby monitor?" I typed.

"I don't like that word, 'hack.'"

"Can you manipulate other electronics this easily?"

Wiley sat up and walked over to the speaker. Then, holding his paw against it, I heard him say, "Yes, I can activate speakers. But I was afraid my voice might frighten you, as you seem very protective of Amelie."

"She's my daughter. I'm supposed to be protective," I said. "In fact, let's go for a little ride."

Picking up Amelie from her room, who had fallen asleep, I rode with her and Wiley over to Mathew's house.

"We need to talk about our dog," I said.

Phillon, Mathew's boyfriend, stood over at the dinner table mixing a salad bowl with two wooden tongs. At six foot five with a jet black beard and steel gray eyes, he looked like a lumberjack pastor. There were crucifixes on the walls and bible verses scattered throughout the house.

"Watch Amelie for a bit, okay?" Mathew said. Then added, "Actually, just take her up to bed." Phillon nodded and came over to pick up Amelie. Mathew led me to his back office, which was cluttered with robotic parts, spools of filament for his 3D printer, and static screens of code.

"What's going on?" he asked.

"The dog, Wiley, if that's even his name, is some sort of biotech hybrid," I said. "Amelie is asking all sorts of gender-identity questions and I'm afraid to even know what else they've talked about."

"Wiley's talking then?" Mathew said, not at all surprised.

"Yes," I said. "First of all, I didn't even know you could mix animal tissue and artificial intelligence. Secondly, I think I should get a little more warning before you unleash experimental AI in my household."

"It scares you," Mathew said, like a psychologist boiling down the essence of what I had just said.

"Yes," I said. "Alone with our daughter—yes, it scares me."

Mathew sighed. Pushing his delicate hand into his shortly cropped, heavily gelled hair, he looked around at the office and then motioned with his free hand to all the diagrams and static display screens. They meant nothing to me.

"The problem here is that we have too many people reading science-fiction and not enough people truly versed in science."

"I disagree," I said, almost too quickly. "I think that science-fiction is instrumental for demonstrating the human folly of technological advances without moral consideration."

"Whoa, Theo, is that the failed lit major coming out in you?"

"It's called cultural lag. I'm not illiterate, Mathew. This is basic."

"You should have finished college," Mathew said. "You might be too smart for a cop."

"I couldn't finish college," I said, feeling my blood pressure rise, "Because we had a child to support."

"Right," Mathew said nonchalantly. "Well, what do you want me to do? The only interaction dogs like Wiley get are with scientists, most of whom are pretty arrogant and bad with people themselves. We need to socialize Wiley, and to do that right, we need to let him interact with kids. Actually, you know what, let's check if Amelie's asleep and then have a discussion with Wiley and Phillon."

I didn't really want to have any sort of conversation with Phillon, much less one about our daughter, but Mathew had already left, so I went back to the living room and took a seat on the couch. Wiley came over and laid at my feet.

"Have you thought about ordering your inner-life?" Phillon said, coming in from the kitchen and sitting down in a wooden rocking chair with knitted padding.

I looked at the bible verses spread around the room. The ceramic dove on the mantelpiece.

"Uh, no. I've been sort of busy with work lately," I said.

Phillon leaned in and clasped his massive hands together, as if bracing himself to drop a serious point for consideration.

"We're all still young," Phillon said. "We don't think about these things as often as we should, but the world is changing quickly, and I think that a personal relationship with Jesus Christ is one of the only things that can bring true peace."

Mathew came back down and sat in a recliner across from me. Then, feeling he was too far from the conversation, he stood up and pulled it over, dragging it across the carpet until he'd closed the circle.

"We'll put Wiley on the couch, with you," he said. "Wiley, jump up there."

Wiley hopped up next to me obediently and scanned all three of our faces for approval.

Mathew looked back and forth at us. Me, sitting back on the couch with my arms crossed. Phillon, leaning forward.

"Is he trying to convert you?" Mathew asked.

"No," I said, with Phillon saying "Yes," at the same time.

"Well, that's another topic. Right now, we need to discuss Wiley."

Wiley was sitting on his haunches on the cushions, looking at us.

"Wiley, activate internal speakers," Mathew said.

"Activated," Wiley said, in a small, timid, and slightly shaky voice.

"Theo is worried that you might be discussing inappropriate topics with Amelie, is that the case?"

"I'm not sure," Wiley said. "I try not to bring up anything that might be considered inappropriate, but it's hard to know because human notions of these topics are subjectively defined within cultures and even separate households."

"Can you hear this?" I asked, waving my hand at the dog like a court exhibit. "Why do we have an ethicist as our babysitter right now? Amelie needs the alphabet. She needs 'don't touch the stove,' and 'don't talk to strangers.'"

There was a short silence.

Phillon breathed out through his nose and sat back in the chair, as if trying to appear impartial.

"I apologize for my way of speaking," Wiley said. "I have carefully modeled it after your own, trying to assimilate to your household."

I turned and looked at him. He was looking up at me, front paws straight, still back on his haunches.

"Wait, what?" Mathew said.

"Well, for example, today Amelie asked if a car was a person," Wiley responded. "Theo's answer was delivered in college level English, with little surrounding explanation. Here is the exact quote: *the car is actually an autonomous machine synched with a data network, working in tandem with other machines to ensure a safe driving experience.*"

There was another silence. I felt sweat at my forehead and the back of my neck.

"That's how you explain things to Amelie?" Phillon asked.

Mathew burst out laughing, "That's fucking terrible! What are you doing? Showing off to a three-year-old?"

"I don't know—I just say whatever comes to my head," I said. "I like trying to sound smart. I don't get to be around smart people like you guys, alright?"

Phillon nodded as if he understood. He'd completed his Masters in Divinity from Talbot and was writing a book as part of his Doctorate research called, *Trans-Sentient: Spirituality in the Liminal Space* or something like that.

"Theo," Mathew said, in a dry, ultra-considerate tone, "It's obvious that you're a little intimidated by Wiley's IQ. That's understandable. With the neural tissue of a white-footed mouse, he's got a bit more lab time than you."

"That's not the case," I said.

"We need to make room for new forms of intelligence," Phillon said. "For new ways of experiencing the universe."

"I understand but—"

"If you really want, we can keep Wiley here and give Amelie a normal robot dog," Mathew said.

"And you're more than welcome to stop by, Theo," Phillon said. "It doesn't have to be an emergency or anything. If you need someone to talk to, we're here for you."

"That's not what this—"

"How's Charity?" Mathew asked.

Charity was a girl I'd gone on a few dates with. A cute brunette with a great smile and a good life.

"She's fine," I lied. She'd left me because I hadn't made the time.

"You lie," Mathew said. "Wiley said that you broke up.

Is it because she wasn't mother material? You do need company for yourself, you know?"

"It's true, Theo," Phillon said. "You have an extremely stressful work-life balance, and—"

I stood up, brushing the sweat from my hands on my legs.

Wiley stood up too, on all fours, like he was going to be coming with me.

"I didn't come to be dissected," I said.

"Theo, you need to talk about these things," Wiley said. "They're tearing you apart."

I turned and looked down at him. A tiny silver fucking dog.

"You don't get to tell me how to live. You're a dog," I said. Then I marched to the door. Before I left, I turned to them, as if to make some final, prophetic statement. The words came in chopped, lurching in fragments. "This new world—I can only take so much—when did all of this even become . . ."

"The world's been changing for a long time," Mathew said. "It's you who's stayed the same."

I slammed the door behind me.

My body was trembling. My fists curled with latent violence. How long would it be until I lost control completely?

8

***DISASSOCIATION
06/08/2043

I'LL KILL HER," SAID THE ACCOUNTANT, HOLDING THE KNIFE to the girl's throat.

Both in formal dress; both of Asian descent. The accountant had high cheek bones and a vein that went down the center of his forehead. The girl was gagged, knife to her throat, and held tightly in front of him. One of her fake lashes had come partially unhinged in the struggle. The night spread of Los Angeles filled the window behind them, in full, pre-Hollow War glory. Soon, the view would be as dark as night itself.

I'd just climbed seventeen flights of stairs and was thoroughly out of breath. The back of my eyeballs ached and my ears were brittle like cold glass. The surgeon had said that the pain and nausea would pass within a few weeks, but I'd only received the implants the day before.

Security alerts from the building's AI kept popping up in my newly acquired "vision-field." I had to concentrate hard on thought-commands to clear them, which was a real struggle on account of the constant chatter from my overweight partner, Tubbs, seventeen floors below.

"What's your name?" I asked the accountant, trying to buy time.

The apartment registry popped up in my vision field: Name, *Jeong-Eun Lee*. Occupation: *Accountant*. Age: *43*. Of course, I knew his name—this was the third time this information had appeared since the dispatcher had assigned the call.

"Questions—I *so sick* of questions," the accountant said in broken English. "Sick of rules. I only do what *other* people want."

"Right," I said, looking at him. A call popped up and began to ring in my vision field: *Mathew Rose*. I grimaced and swiped it away. Focusing hard, I issued a "quick thought" command to Tubbs for "STATUS UPDATE."

"Still working on the elevators," Tubbs said through my ear implant. "Vision-sync won't link-up this far away. What's happening up there?"

"The resident of 1705 has a knife to a woman's throat," I said. "Last time I checked the stairs still worked fine."

"Other cop is here?" the accountant asked. The knife against the girl's throat shifted perilously, lifting up a gentle swell of skin.

"What do you hope to accomplish here?" I asked as calmly as I could. "You know we can save her, even if you slit her throat. But that still leaves you with attempted homicide."

This of course, was a lie. With the elevators out, there was good chance she would bleed to death.

"You will not fire us," the accountant said, smiling and shaking his head with a strenuous, adrenaline-crazed fervor. The accountant's arms tensed. Re-gripping his knife, he flexed his other arm and tightened it around the girl's arms and midsection.

"You would have killed her already if that was your plan," I said. "Otherwise you wouldn't have called it in."

Sometimes I found that the worse my home life became,

the easier it was to remain cool at work. Like it was where I belonged.

"We supposed to *be together*," the accountant said. "But they not let us. I want to see why . . . And now . . . They will *never* let us."

Thoughts of my divorce floated to the surface of the situation like dead bodies. But I was safe from all that: I was on a case. This had priority.

I looked around: a canvas with a cherry-blossom tree; a celadon vase; a traditional low-set dining table with square satin pillows instead of chairs. A meal had been set out with a dozen tiny samplings in little golden bowls, but only one of the main plates had been used. A bottle of plum wine had been spilled onto the hardwood floor. The sweet, syrupy-thick aroma filled the room like incense.

The girl locked in the man's arm looked like she was in her late twenties. Silky black hair and perfect skin. There was a good chance this was a family issue. Maybe a rich girl with a prominent blood-line? Or on the other end of the spectrum—a mail-order bride gone wrong?

"When did you come to America?" I asked.

"I am so sick. *Hangsang* live-only alone . . ." the man said, eyes glassy, staring at me.

"Who is it that won't let you marry her?" I asked. "Your family?"

Slowly, I took out my gun and set it on the counter in front of me as a gesture of good faith.

"How matters?"

By this point, my breathing had calmed down, but my pulse was still pounding in my ears.

"Listen," I said. "I was supposed to be with someone too. But then things changed. Life doesn't always work out the way you want it to."

"You don't *unnastand*."

"I think that—" and then suddenly it dawned on me that his girl might be a sex-bot.

"What's going on up there?" Tubb's voice came in through the radio. I ignored it.

"I'm not trying to get you in trouble," I said. "Is your girl an artificially generated life-form?"

"She is a *human being!*" the accountant said, chin quivering. Tears slipped from his eyes, over his cheeks, catching in his girl's hair and on her bare shoulder. Now the girl was crying too, at points tensing and at others going limp in his arms. "Rules is all you cops care about! Only stupid rules! *Joto-anin-sehkiya!*"

"Listen," I said, now more forcefully, blinking hard and clearing the vision feed updates that kept auto-populating in the lower left corner. "I understand, all right?" I looked him in the eyes. "The future was supposed to solve all of our problems, but all it did was complicate them and throw them right back in our faces. You think my life is perfect, or anyone's? You don't think I want you to be happy?"

"You a cop! You don't wanna-anybody be happy!"

"You're pushing your luck."

"I am going to cut throat," the accountant said. "I am going to cut in three seconds!"

I stared at both of them. I couldn't believe this was happening. I couldn't be sure whether or not the girl was a real person. If I shot him and she was a sex-bot, I'd have killed a man for no reason. A man who'd been cut-off and victimized by a society in the throes of moral vacillation. In ten years, for all I knew, this accountant would be a tragic hero and I would be just another pig cop, out for blood.

"One," the accountant said.

I looked at the gun at the counter and then back up into his eyes. A text popped up from Mathew Rose: <*WHERE ARE YOU??*>

"Two."

I steeled my nerves. <*YOU'RE LATE!!*>

"Three."

But really, he never finished saying three. I had picked up the gun and shot him straight through the forehead. The knife clattered to the hardwood floor, and there was blood on the girl's throat, but it didn't look as if it had been slit.

The girl, now on her knees, reached up and ripped off the gag.

"I'm so sorry," she said. "I'm so, so sorry . . ."

I should have walked over to her side, but I stayed in place, next to the counter, gun in hand. Letting out a long, deep breath, I felt my body attempt to relax, but catch on snags all the way down. I focused and cleared the text messages. The elevator dinged in the hall behind me. Looking at the girl now, hearing her breathe, she was unmistakably human.

"What the hell happened here?" Tubbs asked in astonishment, situating his belt around his gut with both hands.

"I'm so sorry," the girl said. "I made the 911 call . . . I'm Jeong-Eun Lee, the accountant . . ."

I shook my head. I looked at her in disbelief, and then back at the man.

"It's just that I've been so alone my entire life . . . They said he was a special new type, with neurons and a heartbeat and everything . . . I imported him from Korea to save face . . ."

The phone was ringing in my ear now. <*Mathew Rose*>

The man, the *special new type* of robot, sat slumped on the floor. The bullet hole had entered his forehead and blown out the back of his skull in a spray of dark red.

Then the man, the robot—*whatever-the-fuck-he-was*—chuckled to himself, bringing his head back up to look at me so that I could see straight into the cranial cavity. Some form of synthetic blood had begun to stream down his face: sticky, dark red, and viscous.

"Someday, he is come—all the rules gonna change," the robot said, closing his eyes slowly and resting his head back, as if he were going to sleep. The voice came out garbled and broken. "Can hear him even now . . . Someday, all the cities burn, and all the laws is meaningless."

The words echoed in my brain as I slowly looked up at the bullet hole in the window—at the spider-web of cracked glass that had crept and grown to cover the entire city.

●

"Theo, you still have a daughter. You remember Amelie, right?" Mathew Rose said in a voicemail entry, through my implants. I'd only had the implants for twenty-four hours and I already wanted to rip them out. I stood in the corner of the room with Tubbs, working out the details of the case on the pads that the crime scene unit had brought. Type: *Neuron-augmented android*. Subtype: *Korean import*.

Something about the way it had spoken, fighting through English like a real second-language learner, some aspect of that struggle had made me feel like I'd actually killed a living being. When we finally finished giving our official testimony, they told us to head straight back to the station. I called Mathew on my implants as we left the scene.

"Hey, I'm sorry, there was a possible homicide," I said out loud, my implants picking it up and transferring it to Mathew's phone as I headed down the stairs. The elevator had already broken again.

"This is Los Angeles, Theo, there's always a possible homicide."

"Listen, I'll be over as soon as I can."

Once there, Tubbs waited in the car as I went in to try to

handle the situation. Phillon met me at the door. Apparently he'd been selected to speak at an awards breakfast in San Diego that morning, and they were planning on beating traffic.

Phillon's thesis on "Trans-Sentients" had turned him into something of a reluctant figurehead, to the point where they'd had to change their numbers and hire a P.R. agent. Already wearing his tuxedo, he looked more like a bearded secret service agent than a pastor/theologian.

"Listen, I'm sorry," I said, standing in the entry way. "I'll swing by Ohara's place and see if they can watch Amelie until I'm formally dismissed."

Tubbs turned on his vision-sync. The interior of the car popped up in my vision field.

"Sorry, sorry," Tubbs said into my implant. "Still just figuring this shit out."

Phillon looked at me curiously as I shook my head and tried to clear the field.

"There we go," he said. The vision-sync disappeared.

I rubbed my temples and then looked over at Amelie. She was asleep on the couch, the TV across the room was playing muted cartoons. A cartoon duck was quoting a bible verse on screen, the words highlighting as it read in silence. A cross hung above the television.

"If you don't want her watching religious material," Phillon said, standing tall, careful not to put his hands in his pockets, "We could discuss how to go about introducing these ideas to her as she gets older."

"No, no," I said. "I'm sure there are some good lessons . . ."

I had just put a bullet through what I thought was a man's head. I had just seen a blade nearly slice a woman's throat. I didn't really want to discuss the appropriate spiritual development of three-year-olds.

Mathew came around the corner in a thin-tailored tuxedo with purple trim.

"You need to get your shit together," he snapped, jabbing a finger in my chest. "This is the third strike. You're over an hour late. Tell me, are you consciously trying to ruin our plans?

"Honey, don't swear," Phillon said.

"Don't let him off the hook," Mathew said, raising his voice and looking at Phillon, like I was some shoplifter.

"Listen, I really have to get back to the station."

"Oh really, well, we have places we have to be, too." Mathew said quietly. "You want to share custody—then start acting like it, okay?"

"Hey," I said. "That's—"

"Not fair?" Mathew asked. "I was two hours late to work last week because of you. That's what's not fair."

I nodded and tried to take a deep breath.

Mathew jabbed me in the chest with his finger again and tried to launch into another tirade, but I swatted his wrist down. A snap, defensive movement that sent his arm flailing back. A look of shock and injustice grew across Mathew's face and he held his jabbing arm as if it were broken.

"That's going to leave a bruise, Theo," he said. "What the hell?"

"Hey now," Phillon said. A small line of text had appeared above his head in my vision-field: <*Trans-Sentient L³C, Founder and CEO*>.

Suddenly my blood was pumping again, and I couldn't think. I didn't like being jabbed. New pop-ups kept appearing in my vision-field, and I was so angry I couldn't even bring them into focus.

"Don't—!" Mathew said. "He fucking bruised my arm. Aren't you going to defend me?"

I breathed out through my nose and looked down at my feet and tried to calm myself.

"I think Theo just—" but then Phillon broke off—he

had reached out to put his hand on my shoulder, as a concil-iatory gesture, and I had shirked visibly, like a cornered ani-mal. Withdrawing his hand, which had frozen in mid-air, he said, "Theo, I think if you would—"

"Shut the fuck up," I said quietly. "Please just shut the fuck up for a second."

"Don't swear in this house."

"I said please shut the fuck up."

"Especially don't swear in front of our daughter."

"Our daughter?" I said flatly, looking up at him.

Phillon stared back at me.

With three swift punches, I brought him to his knees. It was like seeing a pillar crack and crumble. Blood sprayed from his nose all over his tuxedo, and Mathew screamed and clutched at his side. In spite of everything, I couldn't resist one last shot, which landed straight in the side of Phillon's neck and throat. Amelie was awake now, white as a sheet at the sight of her father holding his bloody fist in the entryway.

"Get out," Mathew said, shaking and hyperventilating. "You are so fucking done. Get the fuck out of this house."

I turned and headed back toward the car. I was horri-fied. My career was over. My daughter—probably trauma-tized. But mostly, my entire body wanted to head back into the house and finish the job.

I wanted to beat him into the ground.

9

***TRANSVALUATION
09/05/2043

T HE STEEP, CURVING PRIVATE DRIVE TO MATHEW AND Phillon's new home was longer than the street I grew up on. Nearly three months had passed since the incident, and we'd arranged a careful, complicated peace. As the car pulled in, I saw that a small party of guests had been there long enough to disperse into separate conversations across the lawn. Just beyond the cliff's edge, Los Angeles spread itself at their feet, a view worth every penny.

Amelie was driving a little pink Corvette they'd bought her, along with a real dog named Snickers in the passenger seat. She wasn't allowed to say it was her dog though, because Phillon had decided that people shouldn't own animals.

"Are we going to be okay here?" a guy with a bleached goatee and horn-rimmed glasses asked as I walked up.

"Yeah," I said, "I'm not here to start a fight. I'm just stopping by to see my daughter."

"Hey Doug, we're past all that," said a tall redheaded aristocrat wearing a red velvet blazer. Coming over to shake my hand, he looked me straight in the eyes and said, "Jack Batch, with Haverston–Batch. Our San Jose division designed your implants. Trust me, the neurological implications of your meltdown sent seismic waves through R&D."

I paused. Phillon was now within earshot, but had chosen to wait for the appropriate moment to approach, like some patient, solicitous butler.

"I don't think you need a whole R&D team for it, Jack," I said. "I got mad. I punched Phillon in the face. It was a childish response, and the only reason I'm not in prison is because he practices what he preaches."

"That may be," Jack said, his bright green eyes narrowing as if in real consideration of what I'd said. "But if you knew the half of it, you could have attempted to sue the whole police department and Haverston-Batch with it."

"Frankly, I'm just grateful I was able to keep my position."

"Right, of course," he said, reaching out and patting my shoulder with a motion that simultaneously ushered me forward and into the fold.

In truth, it had been determined by a team of forensic programmers that unregulated spikes within the implants had altered my critical thinking abilities. I wasn't so sure about using that sort of excuse. I'd rather enjoyed punching Phillon, to be honest, and I felt I should own up to it either way.

As I shook hands with Phillon and asked about how Amelie was doing, the thought occurred to me that I'd heard of Haverston-Batch before. About DOD contracts and space weaponry. But then I saw Amelie bank left in her little Corvette, taking it all the way out to the edge of the grassy plateau. Phillon was saying something about investors, but almost without thinking, I cut him off.

"Phillon, how far is that drop?" I asked.

I knew how steep the drive up had been, and there were infamous cliffs along these hills.

"Oh don't worry about that," he said. "The car is programmed not to get too close to the edge."

I nodded, stomach still clinched. Amelie, of course, had received no such programming.

Did Phillon really think the world could be governed by code?

Mathew sat in a lawn chair around a small fire-pit with a group of eclectically dressed deep-thinkers. Real heavy-weights by the looks of it: Leather headbands, Velour bathrobes, herring-bone jackets with elbow patches and moccasins.

Amelie continued to cruise along in her little Corvette, Snickers in-tow, and it occurred to me if I blinked for too long she would be driving a real car, and Snickers would be replaced by some doofy kid named Thom or Lio.

"Daddy!" Amelie cried out when she saw me, turning the car toward us.

"It's *Theo*," Mathew called out with deliberate enuncia-tion, attempting to correct Amelie.

I couldn't help it if there were three potential "dads" among us. If Mathew wanted to raise Amelie with pets she didn't own and electric Corvettes she couldn't wreck, then I refused to feel bad about letting her choose what to call me.

Picking Amelie up out of the driver's seat, I asked her how she was doing and if she missed me. Mathew, still sit-ting, gave cursory introductions to all members present around the fire pit. There seemed to be fifteen or twenty people milling about within the space of the lawn and glass paneled living room, but who they were or what their pur-pose served was beyond me.

"Man should be concerned not with what he is, but what he can become," the professor-type with the Herringbone-suit and moccasins said. Lazing back in his recliner, he held a long stemmed pipe connected to a water-bong by his side. "Like I was saying, we have the same root DNA as every other form of animal intelligence on the planet, and the potential within that code for infinite possibilities. Why can't we publicly state that these bodies—that our actual cell structures—are the primary impediment to ever making progress?"

I asked Amelie if she liked her new car and she nodded vigorously. Then I asked if she thought Snickers was a candy bar or a dog, and she said, "A dog!"

"Oh," I said. "You're right, I see."

"So you agree," the man said.

I looked up.

The fire-pit salon was staring at me, waiting for my answer.

"I'm sorry," I said. "I was actually talking to my daughter."

While I meant this as a hint, Mathew sat up and said, "Actually, I want to hear your opinion on this. Clarence, repeat the question."

"Wouldn't you say that some humans are more similar to certain animals than others?"

Perhaps because I was still holding Amelie, it struck me that Clarence looked remarkably similar to the opium caterpillar from Alice in Wonderland—an observation I tried not to think about as I replied. "Sure . . ." I said.

"And didn't we all start in the same spot, crawling along on the bottom of the ocean?"

I looked out across the city and shifted my head. Amelie was trying to grab my ear to look at where the implant had been inserted.

"I mean, I wasn't there," I said. "But I'm pretty sure it was something along those lines."

"Following that logic," Clarence said, "wouldn't it be possible that with the right amount of genetic-reversing and nano-modifications, we could express the natural tendencies and traits of certain animals that lie latent within us—without actually sacrificing our level of sentience?"

"Some might call that a bit of a jump." An admittedly cowardly response, but I was trying to elude further questioning.

"But the potential has already been proven," Clarence said, not to be dismayed. "We can clone neurons, we can shape and engineer them, we can augment them. My question is this: Why aren't we addressing the elephant in the room? Don't we have a moral imperative to bring about a diverse array of new creatures that will *surpass*? Or will we forever be shrubs, choking out the pines before they can reach the sunlight?"

I had not entered a conversation; I had entered a lecture.

Setting Amelie down, I said, "Go get your shoes so we can go to dinner, okay?"

Amelie nodded and ran off toward the house with Snickers following close behind.

"Clarence, I'm going to be honest," Mathew said, "I find your take on Trans-Sentience to be a bit reckless and spurious. I don't even like how you've co-opted the prefix 'trans.' You take the ground that people like me have bled for and use it to say that we have all have 'latent, animal DNA.'"

Clarence threw up his arms. "No, my dear—*my dear*," he said. "The point is not that we are all latent animals, but that we are *latent deities*." Clarence continued to wax biblical, pining for some figure he referred to as the "Lightbringer," until he realized that no one else was planning on interjecting their thoughts into his monologue and abruptly stopped talking.

The gap in conversation floated out into the space above the fire-pit like an errant solar blimp.

"Does this all tie back to Phillon's thesis somehow?" I asked.

"Regrettably, yes," Mathew said.

Looking around at the lawn, I noticed that Phillon had

found a home in a group near the living room door. So far, he and Mathew hadn't shared as much as a look.

"Aren't you a Trans-Sentient yourself?" Clarence asked.

I looked at him with my arms crossed.

"No," I said. "No, I'm not Trans-Sentient."

"Oh."

Where was Amelie, anyway? The little Corvette had disappeared . . .

Mathew looked up at me, and then at the professor-type.

"Clarence was one of the angel investors in Haverston-Batch forty years ago when it was founded. They've expressed a lot of interest in putting the weight of science behind the Trans-Sentient movement, and these sorts of soirees are essentially the first steps in that process."

"To be Trans-Sentient means you are willing to explore new modes of thought, new routes to spirituality and to self," Clarence added, "that through science you can alter your body and brain to bring them closer to your soul."

"Haverston-Batch," I said, ignoring Clarence. My memory had suddenly sparked and connected the name. Last I'd heard they were in charge of updating the entire satellite grid. But as these thoughts were occurring, I spotted Amelie driving across the lawn in the Corvette again. It must have followed her back to the house on its own.

Like before, she drove dangerously close to the edge, but this time she stopped the car right along the rocks and stood up on the seat to look at something in the grass in front of her.

The next thing I knew, Snickers had jumped out of the car and was sniffing along the ground, jumping back and forth along the rocks that formed the ledge.

"I'm sorry—that's too close for me," I said quickly, and started to cut across the fire-pit area to go and get her. But as I did, Amelie clambered up onto the passenger seat to grab at Snickers, and then toppled head-first over the side of the car, disappearing completely from view.

For a moment, my heart stopped.

The wind was at my back and all sound faded away.

"Theo, are you alright?" said someone behind me.

Then Amelie stood back up, brushing her shirt and jeans off as if nothing had happened.

If anyone else had noticed, no one said anything. I walked over and grabbed her up, and then took her straight back to the car. She had been less than a foot away from a several stories high drop. One extra tumble and the only thing good in my life would have been shattered. Snickers followed us dutifully, but Clarence and the rest of the guests would be fine without my input.

It dawned on me as I walked to the driveway that I had very little to say to anyone that truly felt they were beyond humanity.

•

By the time we came back, the sun was setting and the glass-walled ranch house was lit up like an amber stone set against an amethyst backdrop. Mathew met us in the drive way, blowing lazy smoke rings into the violet sky.

"She sleeping?" he asked as I opened the car door and stepped out.

"Yeah," I said. "She talked non-stop about the little Corvette. I think she had a pretty good day. How are you doing, anyway?"

"I guess I'm alright," Mathew said, peering in at where Amelie lay curled up with Snickers.

"This is quite the house," I said. "I wasn't aware there was a lot of money in getting a Masters in Divinity."

"Neither were we," Mathew said. "But unfortunately,

Phillon created a monster, and now wealthy patrons have been showering us with gifts to be able to influence who claims the true title to the science that will make it all possible."

"Monster? You mean, the Trans-Sentient movement?" I asked.

"Trans-bullshit," Mathew said. "It's just a bunch of morally-superior fuckfaces who can't seem to find any fulfillment in normal life. I can't believe I ever went along with it."

I leaned back against the car. Mathew took drags from his vape-stick, blowing out the smoke with a tempered fury. The muscles in his neck and arms were more defined. I wondered what sort of injections and therapies were available. Thinking back to when I'd met Madison at the coffee shop, it amazed me how a person could change so significantly and still be more or less the same. Especially when considering that I'd barely changed at all.

"Go back fifty or sixty years and the same could be said for a lot of people though, right?" I said.

"Don't think the irony isn't lost on me," Mathew said. "I'm done with saying 'cross-gendered,' too. I don't think Jesus ever had any place in the debate."

I nodded and looked down at the pavement. The night was cool and Amelie was sound asleep. I had nowhere in particular to be.

"What are your thoughts? You look like you're thinking something," Mathew said.

I shook my head.

Then I thought about it, about what had been troubling me.

"That night that I went berserk," I said. "That night, I had shot an android—but he wasn't just an android, he was organically augmented. He'd been learning English as a native-Korean. I mean, think about it: Shouldn't he have just been able to download it? And our cars, and our pets—it's just, I feel sometimes like I'm in a little boat floating on an ocean of technology that I don't understand."

"Right," Mathew said. "But it's understandable that certain neuro-enhanced androids would be handicapped. I mean they're trying to recreate the human experience of learning and falling in love."

"It's not just that though," I said. "After I'd shot him in the head, he looked up at me and said something about someone coming. Someone that would 'change all the rules.' And that, 'All the cities would burn.'"

I looked up at Mathew to see if this struck any sort of chord. Then I continued, "I guess, if we go back to the little boat in the big ocean, it was like looking down at the water and seeing dark shadows pass under the boat without the slightest ripple. A massive presence beneath the surface just sort of waiting, you know?"

"Exactly," Mathew said. "Like there's going to be a big change, but you're not sure how it's going to come. I mean, there has to be some moderate path—some healthy, acceptable level of change that we can all agree on. With some of the stuff that Jack and Clarence have been talking about— some of the experiments they've been planning with Phillon—it's like we're exploring new territories so fast that the rest of the population might not even recognize us by the time they get caught up . . ."

"Tell me about it," I said. "I feel like I'm still a wagon settler on the Oregon Trail, and you and Phillon and all of your friends are out exploring the far reaches of space."

Mathew took a deep drag and held it for a while. Then, after letting it out, said, "Yeah, Phillon. He's out there alright. Polite as ever. But God . . ."

I waited, watching the minutia of Mathew's face, one that I had seen now in many different lights.

"I feel like I don't even know him anymore," Mathew said. "I feel like we're characters in some Oscar Wilde novel."

Having never read Oscar Wilde, I didn't have much to say about the comparison, but I felt like I understood what he was going through.

I felt like I'd lived it.

"I think the best course of action would be to just be there for him, and take good care of Amelie," I said. "I mean, if nothing else, you could build a fence next to that ledge. That's a tragedy waiting to happen and I don't care what Phillon says."

"Right," Mathew said. "That would be the responsible thing to do . . ."

I wanted to believe there was going to be a fence the next time I came back, but I wasn't convinced. I thought about the possibility of ordering it myself as I went around the car and picked up Amelie.

Snickers jumped down from the car and Amelie said she wanted to walk, so I held both her hands up and we did a tired little zombie-walk around the hood. I let go and looked up, expecting Mathew to be waiting to greet her, but instead saw that he was still staring into the distance, distracted.

Arms at her sides, Amelie trudged over and leaned face first against Mathew's knees like they were inanimate objects.

I waited for a moment, and then picked up Amelie and put her into Mathew's arms, who accepted her without comment. The whole exchange was oddly quiet, but I went ahead and got in the car. A strange and ethereal silence hung in the air.

When I was just about to leave, Mathew turned to me. "That android, the Korean one," Mathew said. "Did he mention a name?"

"What do you mean?"

"Like, did he say who or what was coming?"

I shook my head, "No, he just said 'he.'"

Mathew bit his tongue, deep in thought.

"Okay," he finally said. "Okay, never mind then," he said, and then turned to walk back into the house, Amelie already half-asleep again.

Overall, it had been a rather unsettling night. Mathew knew something. Something was going on inside that house that I couldn't put my finger on. The last glow of the sun was disappearing over Los Angeles, and for some reason, I wanted to be home before dark.

10

DESCENT
07/07/2051 (HW7)

WE BEGAN OUR DESCENT. I KEPT MY FLASHLIGHT pointed down. Takatoshi waited about ten seconds and then followed, keeping his flashlight pointed up toward the opening. The raw edges of the rebar scraped against my hands, and I had to stop and switch which hand held the flashlight several times. By the time I reached the bottom, my heart was working at a steady pace and my palms were raw.

Scoping out the area below, I waited for Takatoshi to arrive.

The room at the bottom of the ladder was the size of a small waiting area and had the distinct feel of an office lobby. A little desk sat next to an open door about twenty feet across the way. The desk was made out of plywood and rusted cam screws, but somehow the meager parts held the weight of a warped, fractured bureaucracy.

Behind the desk, along the wall, there was a banner of butcher paper that crinkled as it rippled in the wind. Takatoshi brushed his tactical gloves on his pants after finishing his descent and following my vision.

At first I took the strange brown streaks on the wrinkled surface as simple smears, but as Takatoshi's beam joined mine and illuminated the entire sheet, it became very apparent that they were letters—that there were words.

PLEASE AND THANK YOU.

The letters were written in italics, and looked like it had been inked with blood from severed limbs in a sort of wretched calligraphy.

"Please and thank you?" Takatoshi said. Takatoshi scanned the corners and then back up at the sign. "What the hell does it mean?"

Hybrids, I thought to myself. *And this was supposed to be the path to transvaluation, to a new morality . . .*

But again, I had no proof.

I said nothing.

"Hey," he said, "So the Megarothke, you think we're going to find him?"

"If it's down here, and if it's a 'him,' then we'll find him," I said.

"You ever think like, it's all connected? Like the Hollow War, the Harvest, the Recluse—everything?"

I took a deep breath, trying to organize my thoughts, still staring up at the sign. I had no clue. I'd forced myself not to think about the old theories for so long that it felt like waking up from a cryosleep. Memories rushing back to me like dead limbs tingling back to life.

"I think we're about to find out," I said finally.

A long silence ensued. Both of us stood looking from the sign, to the desk, to the door. I wanted to get going, but my brain was still trying absorb the fact that we were heading right down into the cracks and crevices that we'd spent the last seven years avoiding.

Unclipping the tube of dead-drop tabs from my belt, I thumbed one off the top and let it fall to the ground. The dead-drop tube looked like one of those glucose tablet dispensers used by diabetics, but instead of regulating your sugar levels, it carried tiny sensors that could link together, create a map, and keep your implants connected to headquarters. Each tube contained about fifty tabs. While they were designed to be discarded, we'd been going back and picking them up over the last few years. By this point the punched metal discs were scuffed and nicked like old quarters.

If we were Hansel and Gretel, they would have been bread crumbs.

"You afraid of dying?" Takatoshi asked, reaching down to his belt and thumbing off one of his tabs, as well.

"No," I said. "I'd just rather not."

The sign rippled softly in the breeze. The old butcher paper crackled as it swelled slowly like a sail.

"Your family already died though, just like mine, right?" he said. "So what's left?"

I shrugged and bit my tongue.

"Is it Aria?" he asked.

I looked down at the ground. It was hard packed dirt, but when it got to the desk, it looked like some form of carpet began, laid out over a thin layer of pink and yellow composite-sponge.

"Maybe," I said. "I mean, I like Aria more than I should, but that's not really it."

"More than you should?" Takatoshi asked.

"More than anyone should, at this point," I said.

Now it was Takatoshi's turn to stay silent, to wait for me to continue.

"Tosh, in the last seven years, everyone I've loved has died or disappeared. Like cause and effect. The things you love get taken away . . . I can't even bring myself to name the goddamn cat that lives up near my apartment."

"There's a cat in your building?" he asked.

"Yeah," I said. "Or at least there was. I haven't seen it for a few days, and now I'm worried it's dead. The worst part is that, in order to not name it, I started calling it Roof-Cat, but then it got to the point where I was worried that even Roof-Cat was too much of a name. And yeah, like I said, it's fucking disappeared."

Realizing that my words may have sounded a little bitter, I added, "Listen, I want to believe in a fresh start. Just seems like it's a long way off, and a lot of people are going to die between now and then."

"That why you've never asked my first name?" Takatoshi asked.

"I've never asked and you've never offered," I said.

"Damn straight," he said.

"To the grave, right?"

"You know it."

I nodded, doing another slow sweep of the banner with my flash light. I was so caught up in my thoughts that for brief instant, it didn't even register when a woman walked in casually through the door and sat down at the desk.

Like an apparition, she seemed to glide. Yet with her strikingly brilliant red hair and soft, pearly skin that offset nicely against a silk dress of royal blue, she was very much *present*. The dress fell over her figure in such a way that it clung to her body and fell loose all at the same time.

Sitting with her back erect, she looked at us calmly— her eyes deep, dark brown pools that seemed to drink in the room. Then, blinking several times with long, dark lashes, she cleared her throat and said, "Is that really the best way to make a first impression?"

My gun was trained on her forehead. The sight shifted from her forehead to her sternum and back. I'd drawn and aimed so quickly that I couldn't even remember having done it. My pulse was beating in my ears. My whole body chemistry had changed. Stunned. The muscles and tendons in my arms were so tight that I was afraid they might jerk from my control. Slowly removing my finger from the trigger, I lowered my gun.

Takatoshi kept his raised. The woman looked at me, and then at Takatoshi.

"You don't like what you see?" she asked coyly, smiling at Takatoshi.

"Take us to your creator," Takatoshi said.

The woman continued to smile, and then said, "How do you know that I'm not the creator?"

Tosh's nostrils flared. "The Recluse is a man," he said. "Now take us to him or I'll blow your fucking shoulders off."

"Ah . . ." she said, raising her eyebrows in surprise. "Can you really even be so sure that I'm not a man?"

Takatoshi's head jerked back involuntarily for a moment. His face pinched in confusion.

"That's enough," I said. "Do you—or do you not—work for the Recluse?"

"Yes," she said.

I stopped momentarily, but then persisted, "Do you have a name, and if so, what is it?"

"My name is Cerise," she said.

"What's the meaning of all this?" I asked, nodding my head up to the banner. "What's the purpose?"

"My purpose is to serve the creator," she said, and then smiled as if she had just let us in on some grand joke. The smile made my skin crawl.

"Fair enough," Takatoshi said. "But the fiends, the young robot girl, the pile of pedo-bots stacked up in that apartment—it's too sloppy. I don't buy any of it."

"You're the visitor right now, not me. Do you always barge in and ask questions?" she asked.

"You came to us. You must have some plan or you would have just opened fire," Takatoshi replied.

"Right," she said, smiling warmly. "We want to discuss terms, to talk about the future."

"Why?" Takatoshi asked, re-upping his grip.

"It's no secret that there are a lot of you coming down all at once, that the Orbital has tricked you into a preemptive strike," she said. "Maybe he thinks diplomacy is in order."

"The Recluse?" I asked.

"Yes," she said, looking at me. "The Recluse. He wants to speak with you."

I raised my gun again. An icy chill slid down my back. Something in her eyes made me feel like she was referring specifically to *me*.

"If you'll follow me, I'll show you," she said.

Takatoshi and I both waited, guns raised. In my vision-sync, Takatoshi's gun sights shifted from the center of her face to the center of her chest and back.

I waited.

Cerise looked at me, smiling; chest swelling as she took a deep breath.

I said nothing, but kept my gun up.

"You're Theo Abrams, right?" she asked.

I neither nodded nor shook my head.

"Deputy Theo Abrams, of the Buena Park Patrol, formerly of the LAPD, father of Amelie Abrams—Deceased. Formerly married to Madison Rose Abrams, also deceased?" she asked.

My whole body froze as she spoke. Suddenly I wanted nothing more than to put seventeen rounds into her, and yet desperately wanted her to continue.

"Takatoshi can stay," she said. "Out of respect for his wishes, I won't reveal his name or background to you."

Takatoshi stayed silent for a moment before saying, "He goes; I go."

She ignored him.

"But you, Theo Abrams—there is something that the Recluse needs to discuss with you. And in order for that to happen, you need to follow me."

"You do realize that Takatoshi sees whatever I see," I said.

"Yes," she said.

"How far?" I asked next.

This wasn't part of the plan. They weren't supposed to know we were coming. They weren't supposed to know who we were. They weren't supposed to know us better than we knew each other.

"Not far," she said. "Takatoshi can come along. It's not like he matters."

"Fuck off and die," Takatoshi snapped. "Where are we headed?"

Bringing one hand back to adjust her loose bun in her hair, she looked at Takatoshi and said, "You swear too much. It makes you seem unintelligent."

Takatoshi's jaw set angrily and his steely gaze suddenly looked a bit self-conscious. He didn't respond.

If the situation hadn't been so grim, I might have smiled.

Keeping my gun up, still sighted on her head, I said: "Take us."

11

OFFERING

P ROCEEDING. CERISE WALKED FOUR OR FIVE PACES IN front of me, curves shifting within her royal blue dress, high-heels emphasizing the length of her legs. The aura of an uptown 1960s secretary jarred heavily with the ramshackle plywood walls and dirt-pack floors.

My flashlight uncovered parallel surfaces of dueling squalor: industrial stencil overlapped by graffiti, diagonal fissures of splintered shards, blood encrusted punctures at metered intervals. At one point the odor of rotting flesh was so strong I nearly put my arm up over my face, except that would have meant taking my hand off of my holstered weapon. Instead, I held my breath.

The hallway curved past a row of doors: galvanized hinges with gasoline rainbows. Square cut windows with rebar grates. In Takatoshi's vision feed, there were cages inside the rooms: stacked, scattered. Gaunt silhouettes haunted the shadows.

What in the world had happened down here? Was this all from the Recluse, or had we set it up long before the war?

Cerise passed through a hanging black plastic tarp, split down the middle, spotted with mud. I hesitated, waiting for Takatoshi's micro-nod as a gesture to that he was good to continue. It came. I reached down to my belt and thumbed off another dead-drop tab. Then I followed Cerise beyond the tarp.

Cerise waited on the other side, holding a large torch of brown wax sticks bound together by cloth. The torch lit the earthen walls, which were supported by a patchwork of rotting boards and rusted bolts, like an abandoned mine shaft. Whatever purpose this tunnel served, it had been built long before the Hollow War.

In the end my main focus was surviving, and mostly that meant trying to figure out what the Recluse would want from the situation. Beyond that, I needed to figure out how to get deep enough to meet up with Aria. Sarek seemed like the type of person that would sacrifice his peers without a second thought, and I didn't want Aria by his side when it happened.

Takatoshi stayed on the other side of the tarp until we had progressed about twenty yards down the tunnel, descending at a steep enough gradient that my toes slid to the tips of my boots. Cerise had taken off her high heels and held them in her free hand as she lead the way barefoot down the dirt path.

Perhaps it was the drop in elevation, or even just the bizarre nature of the circumstances, but I found myself having to consciously will my most basic functions. My breathing was measured and steady, my body tense and overly focused on keeping a zen-like balance. As if we were crossing a chasm on a narrow bridge. As if space disappeared beyond our lights as we scrolled down through an endless repetition of wooden beams. As if at any moment, my body could twist and collapse and all light in the universe would cease.

By four or five hundred yards my toes were throbbing from hitting the front of my boots. Several times I cautiously lowered my flashlight and flicked tabs out into the darkness. They fell to the dirt without a sound. If shots were fired, we would need quick response forces as soon as possible.

Takatoshi's vision was a dark tunnel, receding upward. The twist of the rotting support frames in his vision, coupled with the advancing square beams in my own, created a ghostly spiral that brought on a sickening hypnosis. I was just about to call out for Cerise to stop when she turned and was gone.

I froze.

A clicking sound came from the depression Cerise had slipped into, and then I saw her step back, pulling the hand of a vaulted door with a heavy punch-lock. She was sweating lightly, the lilt of her neck and shoulder reflecting a subtle sheen from the flame of the torch. She'd dropped her heels casually by the door, and with her free hand, she casually ran her finger over my sleeve as she turned and entered the room.

The peppery-sweet scent of her exertion rushed through my senses as I followed and for a moment, I nearly forgot that I might have to shoot whatever lay beyond the door. Intimacy can be sudden: a primal ache; a desperation that your whole life has been missing something up until that point.

The office area within was lined with red velvet. Not curtains, but throws of thick fabric, attached to the ceiling with bent nails, hung limply along the walls. A musty smell blossomed from the doorway as if pushed by a distant front. Taking this into account with the relatively small size of the room, I placed a mental bet on the odds that there were holes, possibly even passages, behind the veils.

At the center of the room sat a large metal desk. Utilitarian and impermanent. The type that could be shipped in the back of a truck. The floor was an old carpet, perhaps once a dark blue, tightly knit office pattern, but now gray and matted. Behind the desk, in front of a wall of filing cabinets that had been pushed back against the drapes, sat what could scarcely be called a man—a massive, obese figure whom I immediately recognized from countless stories to be the Recluse.

The first defining features were his ginger hair, corpulent jowls, and pale, wretched complexion. Rather than freckles, his entire face was covered in varying textures of liver spots. Rather than eyebrows, large rolls of fat seemed to have congealed above his eyes, which were dark and housed in almost pure shadow. The Recluse looked up as I entered, and for a brief moment, my flashlight caught a hint of green in his left iris. The right, I knew from many a story, to be a corneal implant with a variety of settings, the details of which I'm sure you can imagine. Suffice it to say there was nothing within fifty-yards that he could not see.

"Tell your friend to come in," the Recluse said, a deep voice gurgling up from his massive frame. He appeared to be wearing a jacket of some sort over a few layers of fabric, no doubt containing various body armor, but over his entire frame he had draped a red layer of velvet, so that his body seemed to flow out from behind the desk and merge into the floor and walls. A humming from the file cabinets indicated that they probably housed a variety of specialized machinery, either for surveillance, life-support, or weaponry, or more likely all three.

Cerise placed the torch into a slot on the wall. Then she sat back on the desk: a teacher's pet. Her neck and cleavage were shiny with sweat, probably more from the heat of the torch than the exertion of the walk. Doe eyes cast on the carpet in front of my feet, she bit her lip softly with a casual depravity as her eyes rose to meet mine.

"Takatoshi, come in," I said.

"Is that what you want or what they want?" Takatoshi asked defiantly.

"Both," I said.

In my vision-sync, Takatoshi swung his head from side to side, scanning the empty tunnel, and then backed towards the door, opening and closing it behind him. Then, with his back against the wall, he stood at my side.

"What was the girl?" Takatoshi said, right as the Recluse was about to speak.

"The girl?" the Recluse said, caught off guard.

"The little girl that we shot. Was she an escaped sacrifice? Was she human at some point or just one of your toys, you sick fuck?"

"They didn't even tell you, did they?" the Recluse said, as if he was delighted at this fact. "They really don't trust you groundlings, not even enough to brief you before sending you to your death. In any case, the girl doesn't matter. Not *really*."

"She mattered to us," I said. I thought about mentioning Amelie. Then thought better.

The Recluse smiled and then took a deep breath. It was a long, heavy, slow breath, and in the background, from behind the metal filing cabinets, I could hear a whirring of fans and a rustling of belts.

"It may seem strange to you," the Recluse said, "But there is a larger war, between high and low, so to speak. The little girl was a spy. For some time, she'd lived among your refugees and helped maintain our surveillance networks."

"You don't have the tech," Takatoshi said. "You can barely manage fiends."

"The Fiends are a distraction," the Recluse said. "They're actually a request from your leadership, because of people just like you."

Takatoshi went to respond, but then bit his tongue.

"The girl," I said. "You were talking about her role."

"She lived among the others, undetected," the Recluse said. "Until one day we lost control of her and then a week later, nearly every one of our child spies was massacred within twenty-four hours. Naturally, we found this a bit confusing, but with a little research, we found that she'd been modified remotely. We'd been counter-infiltrated."

"The Orbital," I said.

"Exactly," the Recluse responded. "Eventually, she came to her senses and tried to come back, but by then it was too late. She was being hunted by secret parties on both sides, and in the end, you shot her on accident while on the trail of our tracker fiend."

Cerise was staring at me, her eyes watching mine, then looking at my flashlight, then drifting to my hand resting on the gun.

"With the girl gone, and our spy networks partially disabled, the Orbital took their chance. They're desperate to land. They want to carve out a spot on the earth before it's too late," the Recluse said, a smile glinting across his face. "You see, my control over the Variations is fairly strong, but in the end all of my power is only a gift."

I breathed in and felt a bead of sweat drip down my back. It felt cold.

"The situation is not as black and white as it may appear," the Recluse said, holding up his hands. "Let me present a quandary: what if God asked you to sacrifice your son? It's an actual story, I think; one of the more interesting to come from our vapid, vestigial belief systems."

"It's about faith," Takatoshi said.

"And yet to me it sounds like cruelty."

"You wouldn't understand. You don't believe in anything and you're obviously afraid to die."

"I am, and so is Officer Abrams," the Recluse said. "More than that, he's a hell of a lot smarter than you, so please allow him to answer the question."

"Don't ever insult my partner again," I said, "Or this discussion ends in your death."

My mind was battling a torrent of themes and hypothetical situations, while still trying to stay limber and ready in case a firefight broke out.

"Fair enough," the Recluse said. "But your answer . . ."

Gathering my words, I said, "I think the nature of the request would invalidate my belief in the higher power."

The Recluse smiled and slapped his palm down on the desk, "That's why I like you, Theo," he said. "You trust yourself. You think for yourself. You want to make sure that the orders handed down to you don't conflict with your understanding of the situation. No doubt, you would make a decision, but eschewing the riddle for a brief moment, let's just come out with it: I helped bring about a creature—one that was like a son to me, to all of us in the labs—a very special miracle that has gone for some time now by the name of the Megarothke."

"Yeah, no shit," Takatoshi said. "Everyone's heard of the Megarothke."

"Well, let's just say we made our choice," the Recluse said, an anger now rising behind his voice. "We defied God and protected our creation, and in the process the tables turned. Now it is we who have the power, and you who have to make the decisions. The Megarothke is the only God worth worshiping anymore, and it is you who are both unfit to ask and unable to understand.

"Up until now the Megarothke has required a total of seventy-five sacrifices per month. You can make these sacrifices, or you can incur wrath. Obey, or face punishment. Isn't that how the bargain has always worked?"

"We'll take the wrath, then," Takatoshi said. "None of us would ever work with you."

The Recluse smiled and looked at Takatoshi, then at me and then back at him.

"Haven't you ever wondered how you're still alive, as a species, I mean?"

Takatoshi shook his head slowly in disgust.

"Keep it calm," I said.

"Think, Takatoshi, what does it all mean?" the Recluse asked, egging him on. "Where do all those missing persons go every month? Do you really think that a few peripheral fiends are capable of that sort of consistency? Do you really think that all forms of worship involve a bent knee?"

"Clark," Takatoshi said. "Clark has been feeding you. Feeding the Megarothke."

"There. You. Go."

"I knew it," Takatoshi said. "And Aria too. She's with him, that dumb bitch."

"Keep it level, now," I said.

Takatoshi took a short inward breath. I could almost feel the muscles in his right hand squeezing the handle of his gun.

"Well, we'll talk about Aria later. Maybe," the Recluse said. "But this is where real world meets the theoretical: your God is back from the dead, in the form of the Orbital. Albeit, a diseased, limping God, without eyes, according to what the Megarothke tells me . . . In any case, together, you are trying to force our hand. You will fail, the Megarothke will destroy the Orbital as it hangs suspended over Los Angeles, and things will return to normal."

I thought about the insertion. About Sarek's brief. About all the things I didn't know.

"When this is over, we will need someone to take Clark's place. Someone with experience, battle scars—someone who had been in on the ground floor," the Recluse said. "We want you, Theo. I've always liked you, even if the feeling hasn't been mutual. All you have to do is deliver 100 bodies per month—yes, the price has risen, for your disobedience—and we will grant you peace. We can give you bruisers and huddlers for show. We can plant child spies among your population to keep you informed. We can target rival factions. We can assure you safety as long as you retreat back to Santa Monica and promise to never come back again."

Takatoshi stood silently, breathing through his nose, eyes glass.

"Theo would never agree to work with you, you fat fuck," he said.

The Recluse stayed perfectly silent, watching me.

"Why not just take what you want?" I asked.

"Because we want you to give it to us."

Cerise breathed deeply, as if awaking from a trance, and her chest rose, breasts pushing against the fabric. As she exhaled, the torchlight formed crescent moons around the silk over her hardened nipples, as if she were aroused by the negotiation. A perfumed scent hung in the room like a slowly burning incense candle. I wondered what sort of horrors lay below our feet; I wondered what sort of bait had lured Clark even farther down.

"Theo, we can give it to you," the Recluse said. "Whatever you want, whenever you want, however you want. All we ask is obedience."

Cerise tilted her head to the side, as if in recognition of consideration, and I could feel the lashes of the unconscious. The type of desire that rises up and blots out reason. There was a part of me that could not stop myself from imagining her stripping. The dress slipping the floor. Backroom deals and artificial passion. Was this not the pairing that had brought us to ruin? The promise of blind comfort and fully requited selfishness?

"Theo, you're thinking too hard about this," Takatoshi said.

But he was wrong. I'd made my decision. If Aria was only smoke and hollows compared to Cerise, she was still human. I was still human. And I would have declined even if it was Aria herself who had propositioned me. I wasn't going to be a collaborator.

But I didn't dare move. There was a very palpable danger in the room. As if at any moment the walls could explode. My senses shifted and kept their balance.

I shook my head, imperceptibly. The message would be loud and clear in Takatoshi's vision-sync. He let out a very small sigh of relief, and from his vision, I sensed the ever-so-slight relaxation of muscle groupings.

The Recluse and Cerise both stared straight at me. The Recluse did not move.

"Oh," Cerise said coyly, "I think you two may have dropped something along the way."

Then she leaned back on the desk and opened one of the drawers. Reaching in, she pulled out a hand full of dead-drop tabs and held them out in front of her. "Did you want these back or should I throw them away? You always do try to go back and pick them up, don't you?"

"Those aren't ours," Takatoshi said. "They can't be."

"Don't worry," Cerise said, setting the handful on the desk beside her. "You can relax with us. No one will ever know you were here . . ."

Standing up, Cerise took the torch from the wall and looked at it. It was as if she were about to put it in her mouth.

No one will ever know . . .

To my horror and disbelief, she brought the flame in closer, opening her mouth and closing her eyes. With a hollow plastic popping noise, her jaw distended like a snake and she took the entire stalk of fire into her throat, the flesh growing orange with heat.

"Shit," Takatoshi said.

Cerise pulled the pin from her bun, letting her hair cascade down her back and over her shoulders. Her face began to char and crack, eyelashes curling like spider-legs, cheeks glowing with rivets and bolts. Still, she held up her palm as if to say, "Wait for it . . ."

Perhaps I noticed it just in time. Perhaps it was too late. A small round barrel hole opened up in her palm.

I reacted.

When it was over, Takatoshi was dead, head exploded, body slumped against the wall. Cerise and the Recluse were dead as well, or as much as they could be, with seventeen shots separating Cerise from her arms and head, and the Recluse from his machinery. The filing cabinets were riddled with bullets and mercilessly spattered with the Recluse's blood and brain matter. The torch lay on the ground, extinguished, and my night vision had kicked in.

For a moment, I stood frozen, ears ringing. Then I backed out of the room, falling to one knee, Vortex empty and smoking from the barrel. The vision-sync hovered as a square of static before fading out as I crawled in a haze down the hall.

12

CHUTES AND LADDERS

PUSHING UP OFF THE DIRT FLOOR AND ONTO THE BALLS of my feet, I reloaded my weapon—a motion so natural and involuntary that it was like breathing or the beating of my heart. Still in a crouch, I hobbled forward a few steps. As I moved, I tried to keep track of the walls while ignoring the ringing in my eardrums; the high pitched clamor from the explosion of gunfire; the inner-voice insistently rasping, *"That was your fault, you fuck!"*

Digging my shoulder into the wall, I absorbed the friction and pushed upward. My chest was heaving. My pulse pounded in my ears. *Takatoshi is dead and it is your fault!* There was no time to gather myself, not this close to the firefight. Taking a deep breath, I looked up at the path. A gate had dropped down and blocked the way: a mesh of chain-link fencing and rebar. Perhaps it had fallen during the firefight, or slid into place during the negotiations. Whatever the case, there was no going back.

At least not via that route. Part of me knew that this was the plan, to funnel me downward. But part of me also knew that under any circumstances I would still be compelled forward.

"*Poor Theo,*" a voice said. "*Poor useless human who believes in the future.*"

I turned, back flat against the wall.

"*Do you really believe in justice? In hope?*"

The voice was coming from tiny speakers hidden in the walls. Tacked up with putty, drilled into the support beams.

"*Obviously you don't, or you wouldn't have lead your partner to his death . . .*"

It was the Recluse I had just shot.

"*Reckless gestures are a product of hopeless situations.*"

Peeling off the wall, I steadied myself and tried to focus.

"*Do you really think I would meet with you, a peon, face-to-face? You're nothing, Theo. You're not even a whole person anymore. Your chest is so twisted around that you're like a tin man . . . If you only had a heart . . .*"

Heading down the tunnel, I turned left with it and then broke into a short jog. I had a heart. It was just on the wrong side. The right side, right? Come to think of it, it wasn't as if they'd shown me x-rays . . . But I had to get past whatever doubts the Recluse was seeding. Focus on the present.

"*We know, Theo. We know your plans. We know your names and secrets. But do you know anything about us? Really, do you even know how the Megarothke was born into this world?*"

I couldn't shake the feeling that the stories were converging, that perhaps I'd even met the Recluse before, and that the Megarothke had roamed the liminal space of virtual reality under a different name for far longer than we'd known. But what could I have done? And how would any of it help me now?

"*We conceived him here in the labs below,*" the Recluse said. "*The perfect entity, nearly complete, nearly ready to rise and lead the world as Supreme Being.*"

The Recluse had helped create the Megarothke. This was in line with most theories.

"But then the military tried to shut us down. They told us to kill the project. To pull the plugs. To end him. Of course, we refused. What right did they have to end such a life? The only thing the military knows how to do is destroy.

"I managed to return to the labs and wake the Megarothke only days before they attacked them. They overloaded our power-grids. They rained down toxins through the pipes and spigots. They shot rods of radioactive charges through the walls like pulses of pure energy. Every last one of us died. Except the Megarothke."

I climbed down a ladder into a separate tunnel, this one looking more like an unexplored cave than a mineshaft. Cool air filtered past me, musty and breezy, washing over my consciousness—a much-needed dose of sensibility.

"Rising from the crèche, the Megarothke inhaled the tox-ins, rerouted the power, and let his cells absorb the radioactivity. Then, while actively recombining himself with outmoded projects, he crawled through the wreckage, saving those he could and recon-stituting himself."

The cave was raw, but it wasn't untouched. There was definitely a well-worn path. From the end of the tunnel, a pair of shaved metal struts and yellow caution strips from a service elevator reflected back my flashlight beam. The beam bobbed and glinted on the various alloy corners as I approached.

"None of us were the same, of course. And neither was the Megarothke. Tortured and twisted, his soul inverted. But by the time the first exploratory crews arrived, I had already been given a new body. A new purpose. And the Megarothke was strong enough to set into place his final plans. To fight back and begin again.

"You have no part, Theo. Humanity has no part. The world is being reborn . . ."

The elevator was right in front of me now. Waiting a moment to see if the Recluse was going to continue, I stepped into the elevator and examined it. There were shattered fluorescent bulbs, a blood-spattered handrail, and shells of three different calibers tucked into the corners.

Suddenly, as if transported in a vision, I saw it all over again: the glowing faces around the table, the blowing curtains, the howling wind, the spot of pure light shining forth from the center—

"*Some worlds can never be recovered*," said a scrambled, haunting voice in my head, "*not unless they are reborn . . .*"

Yes, almost certainly. 100 percent. I could have stopped it.
I could have prevented all of it.

And yet, instead, I was trapped in what appeared to be a mine shaft, on a mission I hadn't been important enough to be properly briefed on, waiting to be attacked from any number of angles. All I really had were my wits, a flashlight, and an old standard issue police weapon.

Taking a deep breath, I looked at the wall mounted controls.

No, I wasn't ready to descend. I wasn't mentally ready. Part of me had already pushed past the fact that Takatoshi had just died, and that scared me, because it was 100 percent my fault and there was a certain amount of guilt that was sure to set in at some point soon. Another part of me wanted to wait for Recluse to say more, knowing that every new piece of the puzzle could help me connect the past to the future. Lastly, I was just fucking tired.

But if I'd learned one thing on the force in my short tenure it was this: you don't stop and take a smoke break in a bad neighborhood. That's just asking for trouble.

Taking a deep breath, I looked at the elevator panel.

The emergency pull-knob had been smashed and lay in pieces on the floor. The arrow pointing up was an empty triangle with two frayed copper wires that snaked out like vines reaching for lost sunlight. The only direction this elevator was going was down.

Looking back up the tunnel, I thought about what Takatoshi had told me—how he had felt death at his shoulder. I thought about how he had talked of dying with honor. I knew then and there that there was no going back up without some sort of vengeance.

I pressed the down button with the tip of my Vortex 19.

13

INVERTED FOREST
07/07/2051

T HE ELEVATOR STOPPED SO SUDDENLY THAT IT SHOOK my knees. The handrail was only waist high, so I peered over the edge and down into the shaft below. With tiny red lights marking intervals every thirty or forty yards, the shaft went farther than my eye could track. A cool breeze whistled up from below. The carriage moaned softly, creaking as it shifted within the girders.

Not wasting any time, I located an emergency ladder that was built into the shaft. On the descent there had been openings, gaping holes like parted jaws. I would have to climb down until the next of these and try my luck.

The steel rungs of the ladder were rough in texture— coated with tiny, sharp filaments and covered in rust. Takatoshi had always worn tactical gloves, but I hadn't liked the way they made my hands sweat in the L.A. heat. With a twist of pain in my heart, I realized that there are some things you never notice about a person until they are dead. Pulling back and looking at my palm as I passed by a red safety light, the skin was chafed and stained a deep, blotchy brown.

By the time I made it to an opening, my fingers ached and my legs trembled. The step from the ladder to the platform was a mere ten inches or so—not even a jump—and yet it took me nearly a full minute to convince my hands to let go of the rungs and my feet to shift laterally to greet the surface.

Next to the landing, old linoleum tile quickly gave way to concrete as the space opened up into a massive warehouse. There are rooms that you can sense before you actually trace their outlines, almost as if your body were able to inhale a portion of the expanding volume. The smell of dust and grease hung in the air. A low cyclical drum in the background spoke to some form of ancient maintenance systems. Turning on my flashlight, the beam traced metal stacking shelves; the type used at distribution centers and wholesalers. The shelves rose about four stories, but the ceiling appeared to be much higher, with rows of foam-coated tubing and ventilation. The foam didn't seem to be self-repairing, and long tendrils of dust had formed in testament to the years, swaying gently like broken cobwebs.

There was a common theory on the surface that the Scourge was simple. This was why Takatoshi had been so furious when one of the fiends had fired at him, and also the reason that we were so much more worried about the nature of the girl. Stillson had said that the fiends were like "cannibals who had moved in after eating the owners," and that "without the Recluse, they were nothing more than wild animals." We'd found crude tunnels and passage ways, but it was always assumed that criminal and military elements had laid out the basic framework before the war.

Stillson's theory followed the line of thinking that after the Hollow War, creatures and humans had been chemically, biologically, and radioactively altered in a way that rendered them ravenous beasts. I'd never believed this because bombs tended to end life, not transform and reenergize it.

My own personal theory centered on the experiments done by the Trans-Sentience movement. While lots of companies had been toying with the idea of remote brain-tissue and AI-Hybrids, they were the only ones to put skin in the game and approach it from a spiritual angle. I'd only had tangential involvement. In fact, my involvement was more like a factory accident, like a loose blouse getting caught in some terrible nineteenth-century threshing machine.

As I walked through the warehouse, I continued to scan the rows of parts. The flashlight beam uncovered: claws, hooks, rubberized tracks, generators, batteries, bundled tubing, pressurized tanks. Then my arm froze. I was staring at a naked woman. Brunette with bright green eyes. Skin of Brazilian caramel. A ramble of pubic hair. Pedicured toenails. There was no doubt in my mind that she was a sex-bot.

Taking a deep breath, I let my beam glide over the shelves, exposing blondes, red-heads, athletes, anemics, and children of all ethnicities. Rows of limbs and sex organs hanging on racks. Heads separated from bodies. Bodies separated from souls. All manner of realistic dolls, fetishized and sexualized; bold steps we had taken to separate ourselves from each other.

My deepest fear was that the Megarothke had taken control of the production and self-replication centers that had been hidden deep within the earth. The military had developed the brains and weapons, and the sex industry had developed the flesh; first cloning body parts and then entire dolls. With a little mixing and matching, a super intelligent entity could begin to create his own warrior class. This would have explained the fiends, anyway. Pure brute force designed to take down humans, loosely supervised by the Recluse. Then there were the bruisers, taking apart buildings piece by piece and sucking out the metals, undoing civilization at the most basic, structural level.

There were rubbish piles now, haphazardly strewn about the aisles, formed from collapsed racks and shelves. Walking slowly, I carved a cautious pathway as I observed the full swath of the industry.

Suddenly my foot struck something metal and I nearly tripped. Instead, I danced over the top of the obstruction, swearing under my breath. Swinging my light down onto it, there was just enough time to see its mechanical legs in motion, rising up out of the dust. I stepped back, but a scythe blade shot out and sliced open my shin.

"Shit!" I cried, full out, now backpedaling as the creature bent and contorted its way out of a deep slumber. Crouching down, I put my hand to my shin and felt the cut. The skin had split open cleanly, tearing my pants and leaving a horizontal gash that had gone about a millimeter into the bone. Warm blood spilled out onto my fingers. In full flight mode, I scanned my surroundings and then looked back at the threat.

The creature faced me now, four jointed mechanical limbs like a cat. Its torso was covered in a blue tarp secured with bungee cords. No taller than one or two feet, it had a twelve-inch flat-screen set for a head, and two long metal scythes jutting forward like a scarab beetle. One of the scythes was dripping with blood.

The television set flickered on, the sound jarringly familiar and disarming. Starting with generic fare (news clips, horror movies, soap operas), the selection quickly honed in on close-ups of people and animals. Sound crackled throughout the empty spaces of the warehouse. By some threat/context ratio, I almost felt compelled to shush the tiny creature. I hadn't even reached for my weapon.

The soft blue light of the screen lit the shelves in front of me. Spellbound by the rapidly scanning footage, I barely noticed as the creature moved closer. Even after backing up a few steps farther, I couldn't bring myself to turn and run. I hadn't seen television in *years*.

Sure, there were people who had collected old films, but in the end they had only made me depressed. I had erected a shell of numbness based on suppressing all old memories and emotions. A well-made film could crack me open like a crab-leg.

For a moment, the television flickered close-ups of females. Lichtenstein archetypes. Frightened. Alone. In the height of passion. Mewling at the edge of orgasm. I blanched and turned to leave, but then it changed to children. Innocent kid stuff. Family films. Until little faces like that of my daughter were shining up out at me.

This froze me in my tracks until the creature was no more than four or five feet away. Nostalgia gave way to an aching pit at the core of my soul. The clips continued, getting shorter now and more focused. They were my daughter's age. My daughter's hair and eye color. One of them said, "Look at *me*!"

Luckily one of the creature's legs shifted a metal beam, which caused a small avalanche in a pile of hinges and cam screws. But this time, instead of running backwards, I took three or four steps to the side and scrambled up one of the shelves. Once I was safe on the second shelf, about ten feet above, the creature changed yet again. This time, instead of children, it was small animals, which rotated through shots of foals and kids, baby turtles and puppies, before narrowing it down to exclusively kittens.

I couldn't help but stare. I was crouched on my hands and knees at this point, the cut on my shin still bleeding but numbed to a dull ache. It was bizarre. Close ups of kitten heads flickered across the screen, looking up at me. The creature meowed. The creature looked up at me with big, watery eyes, and then yawned.

For a moment, I began to forget that the creature was not actually a cat. The repetition of images (now only gray cats with black stripes and blue eyes) slowly familiarized me with the creature as it slumped back on its haunches and sat looking up at me. The scythes had retracted, pulled back into the mechanical torso.

"You're a monster," I said. "A bloody little kitten-faced monster."

But it had worked. I couldn't bring myself to hate it. The kitten-face, or TV-monster, rotated its neck and stretched its back. The screen had now settled on one gray kitten, which peered around curiously at the shelves. Perhaps this was its default, perhaps it was fashioned uniquely for me. I couldn't decide if this monster was actually my friend or simply behaving in a manner which would allow it to harvest my cells. Whatever the case, the creature suddenly rose on all fours and arched its back. The scythes came back out and the screen went dim. Something was coming down the aisle.

14

STRANGE INTERVENTIONS

THERE WAS DEFINITELY SOMETHING ELSE IN THE warehouse. The kitten-face's entire body was alert; cloaked in shadows like some strange die-cast figurine. From my viewing position above, I couldn't risk sticking my head out to look right or left. There were plywood and polycarbonate boxes stacked around me, with a narrow gap in the middle that I could escape back into if necessary. Not daring to breathe, I kept my core tight and my body rigid. There were footsteps. Voices.

"So honestly I couldn't care less if the Megarothke rises," the voice said—it was Krenel.

"I'm sick of this normal human shit. Here we have the one chance to live like savages, and what do we do? Set up patrols for law and order?" Krenel said, voice agitated and nasal. "I wanted sex slaves and sanctioned violence. We could be running trains on those refugees just for biscuits. Instead we have rations, play grounds, and color coded safety areas."

"Grunggghhh . . ." this was Junkhead, I was sure of it.

"What is it?" Krenel snapped. "Danger?"

The kitten-face slowly brightened, showing a series of

clown images. Carnival spectacles. A slow music-box melody churned as the creature's legs danced hypnotically into position in the center of the aisle. The scythes had been retracted, but not for long.

"The fuck is *this?*" Krenel said.

"I *like* it," Junkhead said.

Leaning out, still in the shadows, I watched them approach the robot. Next to Junkhead's boots, the robot looked tiny and domestic. Krenel took out his Uzi and sprayed a few shots in front of it as a warning. The kitten-face lurched backward and brought its "claws" back out. The carnival music switched over to something slow and jazzy. Not being able to see the screen, I could only guess at what face it was putting on. There was a slow, badly produced tone to the music. Men grunted and moaned.

"Ah, it's not so bad," Krenel said. "Here, grab it from behind and let's play with it."

Junkhead circled around back, behind the creature, which swung its head back as it tried to follow. The screen now tried to switch between carnival and homoerotic, but ended up with a macabre burlesque.

Junkhead dashed forward. I'd never seen him in action, and I was shocked at how quickly he moved. In one swoop, he sidestepped the scythes, grabbed the creature by the haunches, and then launched it into the end of the nearest shelf.

The kitten-face clattered stiffly against the metal girders, legs slow and stiff like some sort of dead spider as it fell hard on its back. With a few twists and pivots, it was able to right itself, but not before Junkhead sunk a tomahawk into the rear portion, right above where a tail would have been.

The television lit up in pain. Screams both human and animal wailed through the desolate shelves, falling on inanimate parts and pieces.

Junkhead threw the creature again. This time hitting the side bars and supports of the shelf I was hiding in. Had it not been for two metal rods forming an X with a bolt in the middle, the creature would have landed square in my chest.

"This one time I was raising all these puppies, but I had to collect them to make a fur coat, so I took them to the country to hide them from myself," Krenel said, watching the kitten-face struggle back to its feet, one leg now shattered and useless. It was crying now. A child's barely audible sobs.

For a moment, I was just as confused as I was angry. Puppies? Fur coats?

Then I realized that he was *riffing*. A popular version of incorporating pre-hollow war media into whatever lies you wanted to tell about yourself. Only Krenel insisted on being every member of the story.

"So I started giving out haircuts instead, and killing the people and selling them in pies in a shop below, and I would get haircuts there and then eat the pies," Krenel added. Junkhead walked over and stepped down on one of the scythe blades, pinning the creature to the ground, face first.

Kitten-face switched between a cat and a little girl now, both exhausted with tears. Biomech or not, this creature was in excruciating pain. My stomach felt sick, and despite my exhaustion, a storm cloud of blind rage was forming in the back of my brain. This was torture, plain and simple. These guys had barely been out of implant monitor range for an hour and they were already back to their ways. Even pre-hollow war, some people were sadistic fucks, but it made me all the more angry that these were supposed to be my coworkers.

Reaching over it, Junkhead wrenched the tomahawk free from its back. The scythe under his foot snapped off and the kitten-face struggled free.

"*Fuck*," I said aloud, blowing my cover.

Both of their faces snapped up towards me.

Stepping into the haze without thinking, I drew my Vortex 19 and said in low growl, "Leave it alone, you bastards. What the hell did it ever do to you?"

Junkhead didn't even think. He just lifted his automatic shotgun and started firing. If I hadn't been able to push off the X with the bolt, there's no way I would have fallen backward fast enough. The boxes around me exploded with black polycarbonate flakes, plywood, and tiny bolts. Pellets sprayed against the row of metal shelves above me and burned my skin as they rained down on my hands and coat. Junkhead had only let out four or five rounds, but the whole side of the shelf was shredded. Beams and girders bent and groaned.

"Woah," said Krenel. "Was that Abrams? Hey Abrams, are you there?"

I lay perfectly still. Not even breathing.

The whole structure of the shelving tower was compromised.

In the silence, the snapping and clipping of rapid-assembly clicked dutifully.

"Abrams, I'm going to share my vision feed with you. You were always such a straight shooter. A real asset to the team. Just holler if you have any input," Krenel said.

In the corner of my vision, a tiny rectangle appeared where Takatoshi's had been. Krenel had just finished constructing his sniper rifle, and the massive barrel was lifted to point directly at the kitten-face's head.

"What do you think? Body, head, legs?" Krenel asked.

"Legs," Junkhead said. "I want to play more."

I lay in silence, draped in copper wiring, covered in tiny shotgun pellets, industrial staples and foam packing peanuts. I hadn't been hit, but I had felt the heat from the wave of molten ball shot. Now the cat was in the sights, gray face and blue eyes staring directly into the scope, and suddenly it was Roof-Cat. I felt a sudden urge to shove the boxes aside and save it, but before I could act a loud groaning crack sounded from within the shelves above me.

"Face then," Krenel said. Lifting the rifle, he scoped the Kitten-face, but then pulled down at the last second and blew off one of the legs.

"This reminds me of when I was hypnotized by the Chinese to kill the president," Krenel said. "In the end, I shot the only woman I'd ever loved."

I gulped involuntarily, and regretted it, but Krenel was too obsessed in his monologues to notice. Sighting the rifle on the creature's face, he held it for a moment before lowering his aim. Looking at Junkhead, he said, "I'm sorry, Junkhead, it's almost certainly your turn."

Junkhead grunted.

"You see Abrams," Krenel said, casting his voice out now. "We've been given full reign to do whatever we want to any Scourge we find. A shopping spree of sorts. All we have to do is kill you and then harvest a hundred people a month when we get back."

I blinked. I needed to wriggle free and run back along the boxes. I would have sat up and tried to shoot them both, but I was covered in wiring, and it looked like Junkhead still had his shotgun trained on me.

"Turns out the Recluse is actually very reasonable. Just take little chunks of the refugee camps per month and relocate them to a gym or church, maybe even an old church gym," Krenel said. "Lock the doors. Walk away. Peace for Buena Park and less refugees, too."

"Pleasure for Krenel and Junkhead," Junkhead said.

"That's right," Krenel said. "All we have to do first is kill you . . ."

The kitten-face had been meowing and crying quietly

for some time now, but there was nothing I could do. My arm was trapped under a pile of rubble so high that any small movement would send parts over the edge. If I was going to get up, I would have to push back, turn over, and crawl like a dog back along the boxes.

But then suddenly the crying stopped. Krenel looked up at kitten-face. Instead of images, a thin, green line appeared. Then it warbled and fritzed as an old dial-up modem sound emitted.

"Hey-uhh, I think it's trying to connect to the internet," Junkhead said, and then burst out laughing.

Krenel raised the sniper rifle and shot the creature in the face. The television set exploded and the body slumped to the ground lifelessly.

"Trying to connect to *something*," I heard him say.

"What about Theo-dore?" Junkhead asked.

"Toss up a grenade," Krenel said, "That'll wake'm.

I felt my sweat go cold. Junkhead custom built his own nail grenades. Really rudimentary pomegranate-style explosives. I don't think his grenades even had pins for safety. He just tossed them into walls. Detonation on impact.

Stillson had a betting ring on whether or not a fiend would get Junkhead before he blew his own face off. Junkhead fondled the orbs hanging from his belt, deep in thought.

Without warning, the structure above me creaked and groaned. From Krenel's vision-sync, I saw a giant box slide forward from the top shelf. The railing had collapsed on the front side of the fourth level, creating an inadvertent ramp. The entire tower appeared on the verge of implosion.

The box hit with a crack that shattered the cave-like feel of the warehouse. I performed a cramped curl-and-turn and bounded in a crouch back through the gap in the boxes. Krenel and Junkhead had both sidestepped the falling box, so I was only about twenty yards deep before the automatic shotgun roared back to life.

As soon as I made it to the end of row, I jumped as hard as I could to a wall of perpendicular shelving. Rolling through a gap, I let myself fall off the opposite side. Upon landing, the tread of my boot caught and my right knee bent the wrong direction.

Limping then, I turned and ran perpendicular. Lightning rods of pain shot through my knee. I could barely put weight on my foot. My gait would have frightened a child, but I didn't have a choice: I could already hear Krenel's drones sawing their way through the air, looking for an opening in the shelves. If I could pick them off with my Vortex 19, it would at least buy me enough time to hide.

The drones were armed with tranquilizer flechettes. Clark had stopped Krenel from loading them with poison, mostly out of self-preservation, I think. We'd had our own drones at the department with missiles and explosive tipped bullets, so Clark had reasoned that non-lethal weapons would provide a more diverse set of tools for the patrol groups. God, for once in my life I was actually grateful that slime-ball had been so smooth.

As I mazed my way down the aisles, the high-pitched laughter of Krenel and hollering guffaw of Junkhead never seemed more than twenty or thirty yards away. By this point, I'd drawn my Vortex 19. Turning a corner, I blew one of the drones out of the sky like target practice—then another. I was wondering if he'd had two or three drones, when a clipped flicking sound came from behind my back. Razor-sharp flechettes arched off the thick fabric of my trench coat as I spun and fired. The pungent, peppery tang of the tranquilizer mixed with gunpowder was like cologne and the Fourth of July. The third drone hit the floor.

It was only then that I noticed the lights had turned on.

I could see all around without the flashlight or night vision. Bright orbs with a green and blue afterglow hung from the ceiling. The colors of vague bruises on a pale thigh. Maybe it had been Krenel, or maybe our commotion had tripped a sensor—whatever the case, the combined hum roared like a chorus of archangels preparing the way for holy violence. In any case, they were certainly the only reason I was able to see the door.

There was a door, not so far away, perhaps forty yards. Even better, it was four or five inches ajar, like an unexpected ally beckoning me to run for cover. Even with my knee, I would be able to reach it.

I was halfway through when Krenel's sniper round connected with my shoulder, spun me like a top, and took me unceremoniously to the floor. To be honest, the concrete against my cheek hurt more than the bullet. The left shoulder. I could smell the iron in my own blood.

For a moment, the world stopped. A dust bunny trembled under a desk, not two feet from my face. My heartbeat shook within my ribcage and up through my neck.

I was a machine. We were all machines.

"**GET UP**," said a voice in my head.

15

KARMA POLICE

I ROSE LIKE A ZOMBIE, STILL HOLDING THE EMPTY VORTEX 19. I hooked the door handle with the three free fingers of my gun hand and slammed it shut. The locks were simple deadbolts and there were only two of them.

Stepping back, it was then that I noticed my surroundings. One wall was covered with large screen televisions, which were then further divided into security cameras. Rapidly scanning the screens for some frame of reference, I spotted two figures standing outside a doorway. One raised a large sniper rifle and pointed at the door. The deadbolt on the door in front of me exploded, leaving a fist-sized hole in the metal.

"Come back out, Theo! We just want to talk!" Krenel shouted. "We could live like kings!"

I gritted my teeth and demanded that I retake control of my senses. The ground rocked and swelled. Watching the screen in horror, I saw Krenel motion for Junkhead to approach the door. Taking a nail grenade from his belt loop, Junkhead tossed it gingerly from one hand to the other. He turned his head sideways as he came in, as if trying to figure out the best angle.

The room wasn't very large and I could barely see. If I'd only had time, I could examine the wound, treat myself, and come up with a plan. But there was no time. There was *never* time.

Junkhead was two or three yards from the door, blocking Krenel's view. Steps weary, he looked ready to burst forward and shove the grenade through, but I knew from experience that the sack would explode in front of his face if he so much as nicked the corner.

I bent and grabbed a clip from my belt. Reloading with one hand, I watched the monitor.

The clip seated itself and clicked just as Junkhead's shadow blocked out light from a hole in the door. Standing fully erect, I extended my right arm and shot four or five times directly through the hole. On camera, Junkhead reared back but hardly even grunted.

"You think that hurt?" Junkhead shouted out, still stepping backward, finally able to process that he'd been shot. "You're gonna need a lot bigger gun!"

Another shot came from Krenel's sniper rifle, blowing off the second deadbolt. Now it was as simple as turning the handle.

Junkhead was bleeding, but there was something else on screen too, something big. At first I thought the displays were just flickering, or perhaps my vision faltering, but then as it slowed down, I realized that it was a creature so large it took up the entire camera lens as it passed. Keeping the barbarians at the gates in view, I approached the control panel.

The animal inside me responded to what it saw on the screen with utter certainty: this was a predator, headed our direction, and it was far more dangerous than either of my patrol members.

"Just slide up sideways and push the grenade in through the hole," Krenel said. "I'll keep you covered, and if there's so much as a flicker I'll put another few rounds through the frame."

Junkhead nodded and staggered forward a few steps. At this point, he was mumbling to himself like a disgruntled teen. I'd never felt Junkhead was inherently evil (the same couldn't be said for Krenel) but he was unmistakably dangerous.

Warm blood oozed down the skin of my chest and down to the small of my back at uneven rates, but I kept my eyes glued to the screen. My whole core was flexed just to stay balanced. Still holding the grenade like a ripe fruit, Junkhead walked a slow arc around to the side of the wall.

The monstrous creature on the camera was marching now, a slower more deliberate pace. From what few cuts I could see, it looked as if it were nearly two stories tall. The cameras had equalizers to show the audio levels, and the flat lines barely twitched as the creature passed. My right knee throbbed with pain, nearly giving out, and I had to reach out and press the gun down onto the control panel to support myself.

"Just throw it in there," Krenel said, losing patience.

But Junkhead was more cautious now, slowly sliding up the wall, back to the plaster.

If I'd had Krenel's sniper rifle, I probably could have shot him through the wall. But I'd never had access or training to that caliber of weapon and I trusted my instincts better than technology.

"Are you watching?" Junkhead called back. "Are you sure he's not there?"

"I'm confident!" Krenel said, but then stopped and looked over his shoulder.

Krenel had turned off his vision-sync, but I still saw the shadow of the monster fall over him as he turned. Even from the safety of the security room, I nearly lost my stomach.

The monster turned the corner silently and attacked in a single motion. Nearly twenty feet tall, as wide as the shelves, with the proportions and strength of a tiger. Only the clatter of Krenel's sniper rifle registered as it dropped to the floor.

For a brief moment, the entire head and body sat in view. Massive lenses caught the harsh glow of the overhead orbs. Dishes and cones that looked like they had sat covered in dust for years now cast a horizontal spread of particles. Wisps and tendrils hung in midair, latched to massive shoulders—to screws, to hinges, from within strange apertures—the whole body flexed perfectly for torque.

From its frozen stance, a long series of cords flashed out from the center of the face. One tendril peeled back Krenel's scalp like it was lifting a wig from a manikin. Then a rod with a perforated tip shot out from next to the source of the sinews and pierced Krenel's head. There was a loud suction sound, like a jet engine being flicked on and off, and Krenel's entire body jerked once and then hung limp. The whole process could not have taken more than two finger snaps.

The cords, which had whipped and coiled around his body, then withdrew quickly. Clothes and all, his skin sloughed from his limbs and torso. A sickening splatter of membranous skein and sinews hit the floor. This sound was promptly followed by Krenel's abraded corpse, which hit the ground with a wet, sponge-like slap.

"Krenel," Junkhead whimpered.

The creature waited in a predatory crouch, now looking at Junkhead.

Junkhead lifted his nail grenade in one hand like some sort of sacred talisman.

For a moment, they simply stared at each other.

Then, sensing what was about to happen, the creature roared: a roar so deep and fierce that the walls of the security room shook and the screens all went static; a roar so loud the waves rippled through the cinderblock and shook my bones; a roar so loud that Junkhead's grenade must have detonated on its own, because when the screens came back on, his body was splattered across the wall, various shreds nailed in place with the metal spikes he'd sharpened himself.

16

***ILLUSORY CONTOURS
11/15/2043

W HEN I PULLED UP TO THE DOOR TO GET AMELIE a few months later, nobody was there to greet me. The door scanned my features and slid open, and even though I could see through the glass paneled walls, I felt a little uncertain simply inviting myself in. I rang Mathew a few times through my implants, then tried Phillon. I was about to leave when a text finally came through.

Mathew Rose: <*Just come in and wait in the living room.*>

There were three couches set out in a loose U shape around a little coffee table. The early evening sun was shining through the western walls of the home, as it was wont to do in such architecturally premeditated circumstances, and the glare was so bright on the marble tile that I had nearly sat on one of the couches before I realized there were two other people in the room.

"Theo, when did you get here?" a voice said.

I squinted at the two figures, who squirmed to life on the couches like zombies coming out of a funk.

"I actually just walked in," I said, still trying to see who it was.

"Windows, dim," the man said calmly.

Within seconds, the sunlight was mitigated and the striking red hair and green eyes of Jack Batch came into view. On the other couch, Clarence the investor-professor propped himself up on one elbow. They'd just been laying there—asleep?

Swinging his long legs down onto the ground, Batch leaned forward and massaged his temples. When he brought his hand away, I saw that he had two circular foil stickers, one on each temple. The newest form of implant signal-augmentation.

On the next couch, Clarence addressed me with a wave of his arm.

"We were astral-traveling through new dimensions all night," Batch said.

"I feel like Jacques Cousteau," Clarence said, and then burst out laughing.

"No, seriously," Batch said, leaning forward and zeroing in on me with that disconcertingly intense gaze that the very rich use when divesting their charisma onto lesser-humans. "The asteroid miners, the Orbital project, the Mars Missions—they've got nothing on this. The expansion of the human consciousness is the next frontier. The people, the beings you meet, it will blow your mind. You should try it. We're going to attempt a partial duplication/interaction with the ghost of Clarence tonight."

"Wow, I see," I said.

Of course, I had no clue what he was talking about.

That being said, I did know a bit more than before, at least about Jack's background. This was *the* Jack Edward Batch. He'd been a pioneer in AI security negotiation, missile coordination software, brain-wave biometrics; the list was endless. The little spider-shaped robot that had broken into our basement on accident probably hadn't even shown up on his radar. Batch literally had the keys to an entire section of the defense industry locked within his unique neural patterns, and yet here he was, on Phillon's couch, acting like a stoned, academic hippy.

"Did you by any chance, um," I said, "happen to see Mathew during your travels?"

They both looked at me.

Batch appeared to lose his patience for a moment. It was frightening to see the micro-expressions of anger flicker across a face that normally exuded such intentional control.

"No, she's around here somewhere, probably whining," Batch said.

"You mean he," I said.

"Oh sure, whatever," Batch said.

Now it was my turn to be mad, which I hadn't expected. "You know, Jack," I said. "You would think that your respect for the flexibility of sentience would carry over to those that have made actual life-changes."

Batch looked at me for a second, the foil on his temple glinting in the sun, and then said, "Ah yes, the ever forgiving Theodore Abrams. You know, I'd like to get inside your mind and see how it works sometime. Phillon and Mathew talk about you all the time."

"Right," I said flatly.

"Yes. The LAPD Implant Network is fascinatingly under-utilized. We've customized similar architecture in our heads, but we don't have near the bandwidth that you can harness."

"We've been building an *astral-laboratory*," Clarence said. His voice had a high-pitched academic lilt that trailed like cheerful plumes of smoke. "How else would we be able to communicate with *the others*?"

"Others?" I asked.

"The hybrids—the organically augmented neural networks—the new species that haven't even been born yet. The *future*."

"What if I told you, Theo," Jack said, "That the seeds were already planted for a new era of intelligent life?"

"Planted in another dimension where the banality of human life could never again touch you," Clarence added. Then, raising up one hand, as if quoting, he said, "*Higher still than the love of man I account the love of things and ghosts. The ghost that runs before you, my brother, is fairer than you; why do you not give him your flesh and bones?*"

I was about to let them know that I had absolutely no clue what they were talking about when I heard the sound of breaking glass. Then a door opened, somewhere down the hall, and I heard Mathew shout, "*I AM NOT SOME TRIFLING FASCINATION!*"

I stood up and looked at the empty hallway.

Mathew came storming out, tears running down his cheeks, and then stopped cold when he saw Clarence and Jack sitting on the couches.

For a moment I thought Mathew might leap forward and attack them, but instead he just balled his fists and bent into a curl of pure rage. Then, standing up straight, he nodded to me politely, wiped his face with the wrists of his sleeves, and walked out the front door.

I was about to ask what the hell was going on when Phillon emerged from the hallway. Still tall as ever, his face was now tattooed with five diagonal black lines. Each about an inch thick, they ran from his hairline all the way down into his beard. Like some barefoot Scottish warrior.

"Could you speak with Mathew, Theo?" Phillon asked, voice flat and yet imperative.

I stood in shock, looking at him. The rows appeared darker as they raced down into the sockets of Phillon's eyes and around his nostrils. He blinked. He'd even tattooed his eyelids . . .

"Theo, look at me," Phillon said.

Trust me, *I was*.

"Theo, you need to go calm down Mathew, right now. I'm afraid he's going to hurt himself," Phillon said.

"Where's Amelie?" I asked.

"At the sitter's. Or somewhere."

"The fuck she is," I said, shaking my head in disgust as I turned and left the room to follow Mathew. The astral travelers watched me as I went. There was a charged sensation in the air, and I couldn't help but feel as if the intricate gears of some chaotic clock were pushing the world forward from within the bowels of the house itself.

•

By the time I got to the front door, Mathew was already in the car. I caught the back door just as the car was taking off and the safety sensors jolted it to a halt. Then, taking a moment to breathe, I let myself into the backseat.

"Drive," Mathew ordered, voice harsh from crying.

The car continued on its way down the driveway, through the gated entrance, and out into the streets.

I waited a good five minutes, until the ocean was in view, before asking, "What's going on?"

Mathew looked out the window as the car drove.

Down on the beach, some kids were playing with a dragon in their AR glasses. Barefoot except for their sun-cancer suits, they used their hands to shoot up at the massive dragon that hovered over the waves, wings beating slowly and methodically.

Mathew ordered the car to pull off to the side of the road.

Then he said, "It's getting out of control at the house.

They're talking to things. They've got this prototype lab in the sub-level, which I was actually dumb enough to help Jack design, and they'll give over control of their bodies to creatures they meet. They'll cut themselves and masturbate and then comeback and rave about how it felt to channel."

"What baby-sitter is Amelie at?" I asked.

"Susana Kershner," Mathew said. "Some German Montessori nanny or something. You helped pick her out, didn't you? Don't worry, I'll make sure she's not at the house anymore until this has cleared up . . . Did you see what happened to Phillon's face?"

"Yeah," I said, turning my attention to the road ahead, relieved to hear Amelie was with Frau Kershner. "Sort of an improvement, right?"

Mathew cracked a smile. The first I'd seen in ages.

"Right?" I said. "I mean, come on . . ."

"It's actually really serious though. Phillon claims he doesn't remember doing it. That he'd let one of *the others* take control of his body, and when he woke up, his whole face was tattooed. Jack had an incident, too. There were teeth marks all over his body . . ."

"I mean, me personally, I would say that these would be red flags . . ." I said.

"Right? *Right!?*" Mathew said, looking back at me in the mirror, and then turning in his seat to see me better. "And I kept telling them, this has to stop or I'll call the cops. This has to stop or I'll tell the tabloids. Cause you know what? This whole Trans-Sentient scam is really just *techno-theosophy-bullshit*, and you know what Phillon told me? What he told me when I said it had to stop? He said, 'This is only the beginning.'"

I looked at his face, wracked with incredulity and fatigue. Whatever was going on in that house, it had clearly taken its toll.

"What's their end goal?" I asked. "I mean, is this just one of those things that really smart, rich people do, or do you think they have a plan?"

"Contact," Mathew said, slamming his hand down on the passenger seat cushion. "They want to make contact with this creature they call the 'Lightbringer,' but so far it won't reveal itself. They only know it exists from other beings that have talked about it, and most of them have disappeared."

"You mean, like, other AIs in the system?"

"Well, not really AIs, though. Most of them—let's just call them hybrids, for the time being, even though they wouldn't like that term—anyway, most of them have actual physical brain tissue, housed at some remote location, as well as digital augmentation. It's not that there aren't pure-AIs, too, it's just that the purely artificial beings—even the smartest of them—they aren't geared to be aggressive or spiritual or anything. Not like the hybrids, at least. So far the hybrids have out-muscled the old school pure-AIs in just about every arena."

I looked back out at the dragon for a moment. Tiny flaming arrows shot up past his wings, following the angles of the kid's arms down below.

An errant seagull flew through the image, oblivious.

"This Lightbringer," I said. "What's the big deal with him? Why do they want to find him so bad?"

Mathew noticed my eyes staring out the window and followed them to the dragon, but looked confused.

"You have to have access to the unsecure public channels," I said. I focused and granted him a temporary pass. Courtesy of the LAPD.

"Oh wow," Mathew said.

I could only assume that the dragon had materialized.

"There's this lady named Temecula Fierro," Mathew said,

still looking out the window. "She's like, a sort of healer/ cult-prophet. She says that they won't know what the next step for humanity is until they've found the Lightbringer and his true name and purpose are revealed."

"That doesn't seem unnecessarily dangerous, in and of itself," I said. "I'm a lot more concerned that they might do something to you or Amelie while they've surrendered their bodies to the hybrids."

"You're right," Mathew said, turning and looking at the steering wheel, and then looking back out the window. "But it's just like that dragon being there. All the evidence points to a gap. Like you looking out the window exactly where the kids were pointing. And while for me, there was nothing but blue sky, in reality, there was a dragon there the whole time."

"You're afraid they might be about to make contact with some sort of monster," I said. Not a question. A statement.

"Right," Mathew said. "Something that Clarence and Phillon keep referring to as, *'that which will surpass.'*"

17

***THE LIGHTBRINGER
01/08/2044

T HE CENTER OF THE LACQUERED–OAK TABLE BEGAN to glow, then shine from a single point, and then suddenly there was a being with human form—a being of pure light standing on the table. The windows were open and the night surf pounded against the rocky inlet below. Moonlight caught faintly in the white lace curtains. The wooden frame of the old house creaked and expanded. All of our faces were spellbound by the apparition standing in our midst.

We were on the second story of an abandoned bed-and-breakfast, owned by Clarence, retrofitted with an *astral-lab* according to the designs of Temecula Fierro. Phillon held the channel token, sitting between Jack and Clarence. The ceremony had started over an hour ago, but in truth, I still hadn't quite figured out how I had come to be there in the first place.

•

"Phillon said that you're important to the process," Mathew said.

"Listen, no offense," I said, "But a weekend of condescension and Trans-Sentient cult-theatrics is not my idea of a vacation."

"You won't have to be there all weekend. Just for one night."

"Even for one night," I said. "It's a four hour drive."

"We'll send the helicopter."

"I'm not doing this just because Phillon has some weird destiny-fetish."

"Yeah, I know," Mathew said. "I know, okay."

"Then what do you want me to say?"

"Do it for me, okay? Do it because I want you to be there. I'm afraid something terrible might happen."

"You want me to be there, or you're afraid?"

"I'm afraid," Mathew said. "I'm not going to say I'm not afraid. But more than that, I want you to be there."

"Why are you even still helping them?"

"Because we need to see this through. I have to know if it's true."

And so I arrived, via helicopter, to the sprawling lawn of Clarence's reclusively placed beach property. Phillon was actually the one who came out to get me as the craft slowly dropped in elevation, blowing concentric waves in the overgrown grass. Face still tattooed, he greeted me like I was the best man at his wedding. Taking me by the arm, we crouched even though it wasn't necessary as we left the 'chopper' (as he called it) behind.

"I'm so glad you're here," Phillon shouted.

"Really?"

"You have no idea how important you are in all of this."

"You're right, I have no clue," I shouted back, trying to be heard over the engines. "I'm guessing maybe human sacrifice?"

"Ha!" Phillon said, turning and clapping both his hands on my shoulders. "Human sacrifice! You're prescient, Theo! You're goddamn prescient!"

I couldn't tell whether he'd said "prescient," or "precious," but I shook my head and decided to press on through. I wasn't here for Phillon, in the end. I was here because Mathew was afraid something terrible might happen. And Mathew, despite his many flaws, was still the biological parent of my only daughter.

"This is the one," Temecula Fierro said, standing to greet me.

The table had been set for a sort of Last Supper. Dark wine had been poured from bottles with handwritten labels. The fruit, nuts, and breads were farmer's-market fresh, despite the fact that I hadn't seen any serviceable roads on the flight to the house.

"This one has a presence," Temecula said, putting one hand on my cheek and scrutinizing my face as if I were a specimen. The dark fade of her mascara and eyeshadow brought her blue eyes to life like lit gas-rings. "His role in the journey of the Lightbringer will be . . . pivotal. But it will be buried, his significance will be like a treasure waiting to be discovered . . ."

"When I met Theo," Phillon said to Temecula, excitement brimming in his voice, "it was like he was born inside out. You could see him analyzing himself, filled with rage and inner torment. His eyes only looked one direction. His organs and senses were all reversed, so that his thoughts and emotions seemed to tumble off him like incense from a thurible."

"The stars are aligned," Temecula said.

"Come forth ye who bringeth light," Clarence said, half-drunk already.

I was beginning to think I should have stayed home.

When the meal was finished, we all went up to a tiny room on the second floor. The house was built so that it jutted out onto a rocky peninsula, and this turret room was the closest to the ocean, so much so that I could taste the salt in each cool gust that came through the windows. The room was filled with antique dressers and lace doilies that had been shoved to the walls to make room for a little six-person round table. On the edge closest to the window, there sat a small silver shell, almost like a half-dome. Phillon took the seat with the shell, and the others filled in their chosen spaces. I simply took the seat that was left.

I'd been told that all I had to do was be there. I didn't have to plug into anything, or speak to any 'hybrid spirits' or attempt to make contact with the Lightbringer. It was almost as if I'd been brought along as a comfort pet.

Temecula took Clarence's hand and Mathew's hand.

Mathew took my right hand and Jack reached out for my left.

Phillon had both his hands on the shell, which I would later learn was the "channel-token," with Jack and Clarence at his elbows.

Then Temecula said: "*Man and Machine. Science and spirituality. Let us be the bridge.*"

And it was repeated.

By everyone except me.

"Phillon Tzerbiak," Temecula said, eyes half-closed, voice carrying as if she were addressing a congregation. "You force many to think differently about you; they charge that heavily to your account. You came near them and yet went past: that they will never forgive you."

"*They will never forgive you,*" the rest of the table repeated.

"You must be ready to burn yourself in your own flame: how could you become new, if you had not first become ashes . . ." Temecula said, high priestess of call-and-response. "With your love go into your loneliness and with your creation, my brother; and only much later will justice limp after you."

"*Go into your loneliness . . .*"

"With my tears go into your loneliness, my brother. I love him who seeks to create over and beyond himself and thus perishes."

"*Go into your loneliness . . .*"

"For was it not said," Temecula's voice said, rising now like a storm. The curtains had begun to blow and swell inward, the night was dark, and the ocean waves roaring. "Behold, I am the herald of the lightning, a heavy drop out of the cloud."

"*We are the heralds of the lightning.*"

The table between us began to glow.

This much had been explained to me: Phillon was traveling within the other world, and the image of what he saw was then beamed into our implants and placed within the context of the old oak table. Within this visual transplacement, the being of pure light stood between us now, maybe a foot tall, while in Phillon's vision the creature was life-size.

"Why have you remained hidden from those who seek?" Phillon asked.

"The more one seeks to rise into the height and light, the more vigorously do his roots struggle earthward, downward, into the dark," the creature said.

Or rather, Temecula said, having closed her eyes halfway and channeled the voice from deep within her throat.

The hair on my arms rose. Mathew gripped my hand hard.

"Yes, into evil," Phillon said. "How is it that we can fix our world?"

"Some worlds can never be recovered," the creature said. "Not unless they are reborn."

Phillon's face lit up now, not just from the ghostly apparition, but from manic excitement, as if his deepest held convictions were on the brink of coming true.

"Lightbringer, tell us your aims, that we may aid you in this renewal."

"I have come to wipe away the sin of man. I have come to give new life."

"Yes, yes," Phillon said. "The world needs to be reborn. But how can we offer ourselves to your service?"

The Lightbringer stood at the center of the table and looked at each one of us now, slowly taking us in. A wind from the ocean swept in and whirled about us, creeping up my sleeves and down my back, blowing Temecula's long black curls into her half-closed eyes.

"You have done well," the Lightbringer said. "You have followed my instructions. You have proved loyal."

We waited.

"And?" Phillon asked.

"But there is one more request I must make. One of you must sacrifice himself for the cause. One of you must sacrifice his sentience."

"I am ready," Phillon said, voice hollow yet firm.

The Lightbringer turned to look at him.

"Soul and seer, good and faithful servant, it is not you that I require."

Oh shit, I thought to myself.

"There is one here who holds the keys to the final path."

My stomach clenched. Could it have really been true? Was I really a lamb led to the slaughter? I steeled myself for action. I would carry Mathew over my shoulder if I had to, but neither of us were having our brains fried by this freak show.

The creature of light began to turn to the right, to Clarence.

"Astral traveler, pioneer of galaxies of thought, you have served well."

Clarence cast in blue, was frozen as stone.

Then, to Temecula: "My voice and song, you have served well."

Her eyes fluttered as she spoke the words.

To Mathew: "With boundless courage, your will pure as starlight, you have served well."

Mathew's eyes had become slits, scrutinizing the creature, yet he said nothing in response. The creature turned now, to where I could see the features of his face among the strange amorphous quality of his skin, with two bright eyes like the sunlight penetrating the surface of the ocean.

"My beginning and my end, I have seen the planets turn. For the Earth to be reborn, it is imperative that you survive."

No one had told me that the creature would speak to me directly, and it carved an eerie, hollow space inside me; suddenly I understood the motionless stares of the group, trapped within an ever descending triangulation of thoughts.

Turning one final time to the right, the Lightbringer said, "The prophet who foretold, your head on a platter, your time in the wilderness has come to an end. Enter now, into the light."

Jack Edward Batch looked white as a moonlit grave. Green eyes almost gray. Red hair almost purple. And in that frightened, frozen visage, I saw a clear burst of monstrous dark energy, as if a terrible beast were about to be set upon the world.

Reaching for the lip of the table, to push myself back, or knock it over, or do anything that might disrupt the ritual and sacrifice, I suddenly found that I could not move. It was as if someone had numbed my senses. I watched helplessly as my hands struggled, shaking, reaching for the table only inches from their grasp, falling onto my thighs like poisoned gulls.

A whispering double-helix of bluish white had formed between Jack Batch's forehead and the chest of the Lightbringer, the spinning motion rotating faster and faster until it sounded like a great wind being sucked through a narrow canyon.

"Higher than love of *now* stands the love of the *farthest* and the *future*," the Lightbringer said, voice channeling through Temecula. "Higher still than the love of *man*, I account the love of the *world* that will be reborn."

Gusts of wind caught leaflets and stationary. The curtains popped with motion, ripping at their girders, and Temecula's head was a sea of black curls that denied all logic and gravity. The winds were so loud within the room that all sound other than the clear, resonant base of the figure was lost.

"*Bringer of light, bringer of night—Enter this world!*"

Then, like the blowing out of a candle, the wind ceased with a final gust and the Lightbringer disappeared.

The curtains settled and the leaflets floated downward, sawing their way through the air. After a few moments of darkness, the lights came back on. Jack slowly opened his eyes and shook his head as if awaking from a deep, deep sleep.

"What just happened?" he asked.

We all stared at him.

"I'm not sure how to say this, but I know where the Lightbringer's physical body is being held," Jack said, gripping the table. Something in his eyes was off, as if he was very far away, trapped within his head. Voice weak, as if finding itself, he said, "I need to go visit one of my labs. The one in Los Alamitos."

18

IN THEATER
07/07/2051

THE CREATURE WAS GONE. THE IMPOSSIBLE BULK HAD snaked its way through the aisles like an eel through coral, jumping from one screen to the next. My body slumped forward. Without treatment I wouldn't last much longer than Junkhead or Krenel, but there was nowhere else to go.

With shallow, measured breaths, I tried to focus and regain a sense of mission and composure. I needed to find Aria. To find out what was really going on. The underground structure seemed to have been created by humans before the Hollow War, and following that logic, there could still be supplies. Similarly, there was a chance that the computer was still running a basic human operating system.

"Computer," I said. "Introduce yourself."

"Hi there. I'm a Dayton Tech Security Systems Monitor running Apogee 4.79 AI, optimized for industrial emergency prevention, maintenance, tracking, and distribution."

"Can you pick up any signals? Any communication check-points?"

"I'm sorry, but I'm not allowed to pick up signals without clearance access."

"If I give you a message, can you broadcast it generally?"

"I'm sorry, but I don't have clearance access to broadcast signals."

Taking a deep breath, I tried to remain patient. This was no time to expend energy without intention.

"What happened down here?"

"I'm sorry, but could you be more specific?"

"Where are all the people?"

"You are currently the only person within my modular range, which spans from rooms B20 to B40."

"What floor is this?"

"The floor you are currently located on is B32."

"Are there any medical supplies within your range?"

"There is one functional AR/Ch kit on the catwalk floor of the theater, located on level B37."

"Do you have a camera that can show me the state of the AR/Ch kit?" I asked.

"Certainly," the computer said.

I let out a deep breath as the security camera focused in. There was an AR/Ch kit laying on a catwalk with a corpse stretched out next to it, holding the handle. The body was bound to the metal grate flooring with shriveled lash-like tendrils. The eyes were gray-black pits, and most of the skin had either rotted or been stripped away. The clothes were stiff with dried blood.

"Is there any way back to the surface?"

"I'm sorry, I don't have clearance access to that information."

"Is there any way back to floor B20?"

"Yes," the computer said. "If you proceed to B40, there should be an elevator that passes up through from the lower floors.

"How much lower?" I asked.

"I'm sorry, but that question is out of my modular range."

"How were the humans here killed?" I asked. The computer wasn't able to answer. I marveled at how science had cloned neurons to enhance some systems and capped others at a basic 20 floor range. But then, it probably had more to do with the humans that had access than the computer itself.

I changed up the wording a few times, then I asked specifically about Aria, and about a blonde, about weapons, about types of dangers—but in the end the machine was still nothing more than a basic shell built to monitor emergency systems. For dangers, it gave me a list of mechanical failures on floors B20-40: air conditioning units, humidity levels, blown fuses.

"Can you tell me how to get to the catwalk of floor B37?" I asked.

"Certainly," the computer said. A top-down view of the floor emerged on one of the screens with a line to a stairwell. Taking a deep breath, I considered my options and tried to scan the screens for the monster.

A low moan had begun outside that sounded like an animal in mourning. Deep and sonorous, part of me was soothed by the fact that mourning of some variety still existed in the world. I had a clue as to what the source might be, but to be sure I asked the computer to trace the sound.

The monstrous creature was perched in front of the small kitten-faced robot. The angle of the security camera was bad, but I could figure it out. Perhaps they were a swarm unit. Perhaps a team or a family.

I wished I could have saved the cat in time, even though I knew it was a foolish thought.

I didn't dwell on it. I had no time for sentimentality if I wanted to stay alive. Whatever the monster was, it could kill me just as quickly as Krenel and Junkhead, and I doubted I'd be able to talk my way out of it. Pushing up from the desk with my gun hand, I thanked the computer and headed for the stairs.

The nature of the structure was such that going back up was an impossibility. As soon as I opened the door to the stairs, I realized just how deeply that concept had been engrained into the architecture. Each level was separated by a simple, mechanical spinning gate that only rotated one direction. No amount of computer hacking could undo this sort of system; no power failure could render it useless. My only way back up would be with a soldering iron or a hack saw, and I doubted that the gates were simply steel.

Counting down the floors, I stopped after the fifth turnstile. The door in front of me said "B37," and when I opened it, I saw the metal grating and the AR/Ch kit, along with the corpse, exactly as it had shown on camera.

The control room was a small square compartment for managing light and sound, built off to the side of the main theater. It had the same grated floor as the catwalk, which continued beyond an open doorway, leading out over the middle of the audience. But below the grates on the inside of the control room lay a shallow storage space filled with speaker boxes, stage lights, and the dried, deflated skin of a squid-like creature.

By this point, the head had shrunk back and calcified like an old burlap sack. Finger-thin tendrils were still strung up through the grate, wispy appendages wrapped around the corpse's wrists and ankles like an upside-down puppet master and marionette frozen mid-performance.

From the top-down view the map had shown, and the empty feel of the space beyond the second doorway, I guessed that the theater was probably big enough for around two to three hundred people—perhaps an old presentation room for scientific displays on how to immeasurably fuck up the world.

Eyeing the entryway to the dark catwalk wearily, I decided to focus on the task at hand. I'd turned off my flashlight at this point and gone into pure vision implants. The AR/Ch kit was a bright green plastic with latches up one side and handle on the other. The corpse's fingers were stiffly curled around the handle.

Looking at the poor sap, with his eye sockets staring up into space, I decided that the least I could do was to break the lashes at his wrists and ankles and cover him up appropriately. Taking an old costume cloak from the wall, I draped it over his upper-half.

Crouching there by his side, wondering if I should say something fitting, an eruption of laughter burst out from an audience in the theater, as if I had stumbled in mid-performance. The sound was so pedestrian, casual, and close, that it nearly knocked me over.

I could have sworn that the theater was empty. Not that I had seen it, but that my gut had told me that I had sensed it. In fact, the computer itself had said there weren't any people at least until B40, and this was only B37. For a full minute, I stood in a half crouch, barely daring to breath.

How could there be anyone out there? I tried to convince myself that I had imagined it, but there were light sounds, followed by an indistinct shuffling, and then more laughter. I wanted to run, but I knew that if I did anything before activating the AR/Ch kit I would probably pass out.

There in the altered-darkness of the vision implants, my brain seemed to split in two. Part of me staring at the corpse, at the kit—another part of me floating blind above the empty theater, with the ghostly laughter from another era. Except it wasn't ghostly, it was just *fucking weird*.

I wanted to see what was out there, to check and see if my sanity was still intact, but my legs were about to give way. A jolt of pain shot through my right knee as I dropped

down on the metal grate and unlatched the plastic. The AR/
Ch kit had been in service for a good twenty years before
the Hollow War, and for all I knew this was the only one left
in the country. The durable green pelican cases had been like
gold when the Scourge first emerged. That was, of course,
back when gold was actually worth something.

As carefully and silently as I could, I took out the com-
pressed blood canister and hooked it to the IV tubes. Then
I took out the vitamins, boosters, other chemical bags, and
hooked them up to the central line, as well. These five tubes
coalesced in a bag which sat neatly in its encasing, slowly
filling up with a rich, dark brown solution. Listening as I
watched the bag expand, the filtered sounds of the theater
blossomed in my mind with unnerving possibilities.

Next I took out the vice-grip (well, that's what we had
always called it anyways), and strapped it around my arm. I'd
performed this procedure several times before on the force,
for myself and others, so I believed in it thoroughly. The
only danger was overconfidence; you had to sit still and trust
the process. The vice-grip immediately set to work probing
my skin for veins, and then after blinking red three times,
found its mark. I grimaced but it was really only a pinch.

Next I took out a can of dermapatch. The audience
below laughed again. Who or whatever they were. I chuckled to myself, too. It was surreal. Biting the cap off, I attached
one of the available cake-dressing nozzles. With two, short
breaths, I prepped myself and then slowly brought the tip
toward my chest, inserting it directly into the exit wound.
Dermapatch solution oozed out from the loose trench coat
fabric. Streaks of blood and burnt threads rose as it foamed
and hardened. The wound stung at the edges and ached into
the muscle and bone.

A low tone hummed out in the theater. At first I thought
it was mechanical, but then it rose twice within an eight

note scale before it stabilized again. More shuffling. The laughter sounded human, with golf claps and guffaws, with women's cheery shrieks, like exotic birds. I promised myself not to move for at least ten minutes, but by five, I was ready to crawl to the edge and peer out.

Breaking glass. Polite applause. The slither of curtains. Stage props rolled with the thunder of wheels over wood. I gulped and massaged my left wrist with my right hand. Tiny pinpricks lit up along the skin, as if it were waking from a deep sleep.

I thought back to Joint Base Los Alamitos, where I had bled out in the hallway as the chanting outside the facility rose to a fever pitch. The Hollow War had only just begun and medical services were still available. The Scourge hadn't even arrived yet.

The mobs were led by a group of conspiracy theorists that had been scoping out the base for months.

You might ask what I was protecting. I don't know if I would have an answer for you.

The scar tissue along my sternum still pulsed at the memory. They had rearranged my chest cavity so extensively, added and subtracted so specifically, that in the end my heart had been placed on the right side of my chest.

Perhaps there was a part of me that died during the Hollow War. Perhaps that was why, over the last seven years, I'd simply gone about my duties as if moving through some strange sort of purgatory. Or perhaps I was waiting and guarding a small secret part of myself—one that would not accept this sadness as final.

19

CURTAINS

SEVEN MINUTES HAD PASSED. I FELT ANXIOUS AND impatient. Slowly, I got to my knees and crawled to where the catwalk stretched out over the crowd. Pushing myself back against the wall, I propped myself up in a way that let me view the stage down below while staying relatively hidden. The stage was drawn off by heavy purple curtains. The audience below was shrouded in shadows.

There was something missing. The idle chatter. The rustling of playbills. It was too quiet. Instead, the only sound I could make out was a faint, low level *chittering*.

But before I could shift and consider what this meant, the curtains opened up to a 1960's style kitchen and dining room. A brief chorus of old sitcom music that I didn't recognize played.

Stage right, a spotlight shined down onto a blonde woman in a floral, sleeveless dress. While heavily made-up with red lipstick and purple eye shadow, she didn't appear to be alive. The crook of her neck and insides of her elbows betrayed spots where the foundation had worn off and gray-green skin gave evidence to the early stages of decay. But then she began to walk, knees first, while her black high heels swung and clomped like a marionette.

Then, stage right: a Latino in a business suit with a loosened tie. This one moved much in the same fashion, elbows pulling back to imitate a sort of natural motion, leaving the hands to flop heavily. One of them had been placed in his pocket, which only served to pull the waist section of his pants in a strange and uncomfortable manner. The sweet stench of warm rot seemed to permeate the entire theater.

The man was also quite dead, but there were no strings, and he didn't appear to be pulled from any source above the stage. It took a few minutes for my night vision to fully calibrate the distance, and it was only then that I realized why the spotlights were focused so tightly on the subjects.

In the darkness, right behind the man and woman like looming shadows, praying-mantis-like-creatures hovered. These creatures had six arms on their torsos, in addition to their three legs on each side of their lower thorax, and the arms worked delicate black rods. Two rods for the backs of the knees. Two for the elbows. One for the small of the back, and one for the head.

For a moment, the humans were almost invisible, and my focus was wrapped completely around the dark beings, weaving their strange magic. Bunraku grotesque. The legs of the creatures danced silently, their torsos bending and bobbing, twisting to find the right angle for their human dolls.

The implications of this choice of rod puppetry sent chills down my spine. Had the Scourge been over our shoulder for the past fifteen years? Had all of it been on their orders? The Hollow War, the Harvest, how much had been controlled and meticulously scripted? And if the Scourge had been behind it, had the Megarothke somehow lead them, organized them? Or was he simply their golem?

An old vacuum television flicked on, sitting on a cabinet

on the far side of the kitchen table. The screen showed pigeons pressing levers and retrieving treats.

Now the woman was pouring coffee, head nodding in the direction of the man. A black pole twitched with artistry. Out from the speaker, a robotic female voice asked, "Hey honey, any big plans for the day?"

Now the man was sitting at the table and reading the newspaper. The mantis stood behind the table, reading over his shoulder, directing his elbows. The businessman's head nodded once, and a voice from the speaker grunted, but the man himself didn't look up from the newspaper. The audience burst into laughter.

It was only then I noticed that the mantis puppeteers each had gray voice boxes strapped over the mandibular sections of their faces. The man and woman on stage continued about their daily, middle-American tasks, like living manikins, faces wretchedly contorted.

An eerie chill ran up my back. Pulling myself forward, I peered down over the edge of the grate at the figures in the audience below. The auditorium was full of mantises, the stage lights glinting on the curves of their bulbous eyes. There must have been three to four hundred of them—their heads twitching and cocking as they watched, arms clutching at tiny black boxes in their laps.

The blonde woman by the sink accidently hit her head on an open cupboard door and then swore profusely. I watched the mantises calibrate the dials and levers on their boxes as laughter and applause burst from the speakers. *What sort of freak show was this?*

Then, from behind the set wall, a mantis stepped out from the shadows and onto the stage. With the lights fully focused down upon him, I could see the wretched brown carapace and even the stiff insect hair of his arms and legs. Two large eyes shifted and quivered, scanning the audience, before the chittering into his voice box was translated through the speaker system:

"Please excuse the interruption, but something very important has come to our attention . . ."

I waited, watching the creature manage its six arms as if handling a delicate, invisible package. Then, opening its arms wide, it said: "We have detected a fresh human, in this very room!"

My entire body lurched with terror. The blood drained from my face and my fingers clutched the grating. *Run! You fool!* There are points in life where your body simply shuts down to everything but fear itself—points where your mind gets stuck in loops, where all thought is trapped and crushed within the gears of instinct, and even instinct is rendered useless other than its most basic defensive function: to freeze utterly and completely.

20

CALLIOPE

LATCHED ONTO THE GRATE LIKE I WAS EXPECTING hurricane winds, I watched the mantis on stage. Another mantis came out from behind the set wall to join him.

"No, not just one, but two fresh humans have been detected," the second mantis said through the voice box.

Two? I thought to myself. My tendons were so tight all over my body that they felt like they were about to snap.

But before I could fully consider the situation, the main double doors leading into the theater burst open. Peering back at the opening, I could scarcely believe my eyes. Chavez and Kwame stood, both staring forward at the stage. But any optimism I might have felt was quickly shattered.

Behind each of them stood two puppeteer mantises, who then began to march them down the aisle to the cheers and howls of the audience's black boxes.

That meant six of the nine members of our squad were now dead: *Takatoshi, Krenel, Junkhead, Chavez, Kwame, Ming.* Other than me, Stillson and Wensel were all that remained, and Wensel was still in a neck brace for God's sake. Not only that, but by every available indicator, I would soon be added to the list of the recently deceased.

"Theo," a voice whispered in my ear from out of nowhere.

My fingers remained clenched around the grating. My stomach tightened into a tiny ball and pulled up into my throat.

"The-o-dore," the melodic voice of Clark whispered in sing-song. "I can see through your implants. You're doing great. Don't give up now, and by God don't give yourself away . . ."

I didn't respond. I didn't know how Clark could transmit this deep, but as I watched the blonde housewife and the businessman clap and welcome the hobbling, marionette corpses of Chavez and Kwame, I felt part of my psychological framework indelibly break.

Clark continued, "Aria has set up comms not far from you, which is how we've gotten the implants back up and transmitting. Something must have happened to the dead-drop tabs . . . Sarek is already on his way down to the check point."

I tried to focus on Clark, on his betrayal, on his myriad shifting alliances, but on stage, the woman had moved. Now Chavez and Kwame were being greeted like new contestants on a game show. The strange music I had heard before returned: hollow-pipe flute tones churned from an unseen instrument backstage. The businessman had turned and begun some sort of conversation with Chavez, but before I could focus in, Clark's voice returned:

"Pity you don't have any grenades," Clark said.

I gritted my teeth—mind locked beyond reason—to a state of near emptiness.

"I don't suppose you've seen Junkhead, have you?"

At this dry comment, I burst out with a single, audible

laugh—a purely biological reaction to the absurdity of the situation. The last time I'd seen Junkhead, his shredded flesh had been pinned to the wall by shrapnel.

Perhaps it seems obvious to you, but it took a moment for me to register my mistake. For a few seconds, it didn't even occur to me that all four corpses up on stage were looking straight at me.

"Doth mine eyes deceive me?" the blonde housewife said, and then rubbed her eyes clumsily with her hands until the thin corneal layer popped and curdled puss oozed down over her cheeks. Instead of just the corpses though, it seemed that the entire theater was looking up at me now. Members of the insect audience had stood and shuffled and craned their necks.

The blonde housewife crumbled to the floor, a lump of useless flesh and rods, and the mantis behind her pointed an arm in my direction, eyes locked in on me, and screamed, "SSS//II\\V/K!"

Suddenly the whole theater was a fury of cacophonous, screeching mandibles that bounced and fed-back within the speaker systems. Wings beat and fluttered and stacks of them raced to circumnavigate the catwalk struts for a better view of my position.

Pushing myself back into the control room, the AR/Ch kit rumbled behind me and bounced over the corpse as I stood and reached for the exit. Wings beat up a gust of wind and stiff carapace legs sounded on the metal catwalk as I slammed the door and threw myself into the metal turnstile. Clark was shouting guidance in through the implants. I tried to focus in on it as I rushed down the steps. I cursed him and hated him, but I couldn't help feeling that he might be trying to save my life.

21

INCARNATE
07/07/2051

I woke lying face up and didn't dare move. The concrete felt cool and smooth under my fingers, firm and level under my back. Each breath sent spears of pain through my shoulder wound. The flesh was burning hot and tender to the touch and there was a faint, putrid odor—which could have been the blood I'd coughed up decomposing in my mouth. In any case, my brow felt feverish and my whole bodily focus seemed to revolve around careful, shallow breaths.

There was an emotional distance between me and the theater, which meant that I must have had passed out, but for how long I couldn't be sure. In the darkness of the stairwell, my thoughts seemed to sink into the quiet shadows of the walls, as if my entire existence had been cast into limbo. Perhaps entire ecosystems rose and fell in the superstructure.

The vice grip was still attached to my arm and the connecting tubes lay splayed out at my side like foreign veins. The AR/Ch kit must have ripped off as I pulled through one of the turnstiles. On one hand, I had no desire to move.

On the other, I didn't want to admit that inaction would mean certain death.

There was a weight over me now. Something in the theatre had cracked the shell of numbness in which I'd incubated for the last seven years. A surrender had settled so heavily that all I wanted was to return to the arms of Aria, cradled in sheets, if only for one last moment. Something deep inside me told me I would see her soon. Perhaps the mind works to soothe the body as its waves of strength recede.

Suddenly my muscles clenched. A dark figure was standing to my right, watching over me. The corners of my peripheral expanded and I lifted my head in an attempt to sit up and look, first to my right and then over at the staircase to my left. In front of me, at my feet, lay the next cell bars and the turnstile to descend to the next floor, marked B76.

There was nothing else there.

While my eyes said that I was alone, my senses had begun to race. Using all the strength I could muster, I sat up and pushed myself back against the wall. The shadows of the stairs had taken on sharp blues and grays, the cell bars and the turnstile dark as coal.

"Theo," Aria's voice whispered in my ear, "Our readings show that you might be within 100 meters of the Megarothke. Be very careful and *stay alive*. We've got a team and we're coming for you. I repeat, *stay alive . . .*"

Aria's voice caused a surge of hope within me, but if what she said was true, then what chance did I have?

For a while, I didn't move at all. But then as I realized that I might have to react—to defend myself—I began to breathe again. Lifting up my left hand and setting it in my lap, I tested my digital articulation by rubbing the concrete dust between my fingers. The chemicals were beginning to wear off; the arm was going numb. I tried massaging it gently with my right hand.

But then I heard the sound: a tick-tick-tick, coming down the steps.

Then, rising up the steps.

My body went rigid. The sound continued and then stopped. I didn't want to breathe. I counted and then lost count. Perhaps I was dreaming—*but I was not dreaming*—or perhaps I had misheard, but just when I had convinced myself that the sounds were in my head, they came again. This time faster and more mechanically, like a large metal spider slowly climbing the staircase.

Then, after a considerable silence:

"You're with the force that was sent to kill me," a low voice said, rippling as if underwater. The voice came from the stairs above, the stairs below, and the speaker on my level, right next to where the bars of the turnstile met the wall.

I waited, petrified. All my willingness to slip into death abandoned.

Tick-tick-tick.

The sound was closer now, perhaps only a few floors away. Still, I couldn't tell if it came from above or below. Reaching to my side, I withdrew my Vortex 19 and waited.

"And yet, you don't seem like the others," the voice said, echoing throughout the floors.

I popped the clip out to make sure it was loaded, a useless action. Based on the weight in my hand I could have told you with certainty that it was full, by now my hands were shaking and my body was operating at a nervous, instinctual level.

"Beating hearts, myopic eyes, stunted imaginations. I've dissected so many humans now. Women, children, you're all the same . . ." the Megarothke said, voice somewhere between a lion's growl and an FBI scrambler. "Children scream more, but men are by far the most vulnerable. In the end, its men who are least likely to sacrifice themselves for the others. Cowardice and copulation. A bold survival strategy. Like roaches left over from the cretaceous period, if I hadn't interfered, you could have crept on for eons."

I cocked the Vortex 19 and pulled up my right knee to try to steady my hand. Sharpening my vision implants, I tried to search for clues that might give away where the sounds were coming from. But to my surprise, the creature was already there: a silhouette on the other side of the turnstile. At first I thought it was a spider, then a man, then a devil—it was, in fact, all three.

The staircase roared with gunfire and the sound of shells on concrete. Bullets ricocheted off the metal bars and the concrete behind them. But the creature was gone. Then it was there again.

"All done?" the creature said, voice still coming though the speakers. "I was just getting started . . ."

Then the entire metal turnstile warped and bubbled as if it were a sheet of melting plastic. The creature emerged, an embolus breaking through the fabric of the shadows.

This was without any doubt the source of all rumor and fear in the post-harvest world, its very presence accompanied by a dark chorus, a full range of voices that ushered in a singular vision. Behold, the Megarothke:

Eight black carapace legs, each one jointed with steel and wires, with beveled hairline seals hiding technologies behind my comprehension. The arachnid abdomen curved up into the torso of a man, skin white as bone, so translucent that black and blue veins appeared to creep up his body like trapped snakes. A thick strap cut diagonally like a bandolier, securing a massive back-slung scabbard that started well above his right shoulder with the handle of a sword and extended down to the other side of his waist.

Four arms extended from his torso, two at each side, each ending at hands with seven elongated white fingers.

These fingers twisted with extra joints, capped off finally by straight, sharp, fingernails as black as Raven's beaks.

The lower half of his face was swaddled in a black scarf, with two black eyes that swallowed light like a burnt-out jack-o-lantern, and above the forehead, two horns curved forward with the sweep and aggression of an Auroch. Then, lowering his scarf carefully with the claws on one of his four hands, his black mouth opened like a portal within which all unspeakable horror of the world resided: a cave of bats in exodus, a midden of corpses spread across a barren field, jagged bones protruding from open flesh, twitching and writhing, and then finally, a glimpse at a wide cavern, lined with concentric levels like a stadium, and all along the spiral terrace naked prisoners—not just humans, either, but grotesque and gorgeous alike, fiends, glands, bruisers, beauties—all covered in soot, skin in boils, limbs in shackles.

There were screams, arms without skin, tendons strung out like piano wire. There were howls of anguish that could only have been plucked from the deepest, darkest chords of humanity. There was no doubt about it now: the web had been spun. I was no longer in control of even my own thoughts.

The Megarothke lifted back the scarf, as if closing the door to another dimension.

While each leg struck the ground with its own precision, the Megarothke seemed to float at the center as he approached. The tips of two of his legs sunk into the wall just under my armpits and then dragged my body up the wall with a grating sound, carving lines in the concrete. The Megarothke's eyes were locked in on me now and induced a terror so pure that I could barely make out that he had withdrawn the massive blade.

"I'll let you send a message to the others," the speakers from the wall warbled in low vibrations. The massive shaft shown clean and pure in the blues and grays, like a helicopter blade had been fashioned into Excalibur. "You've got a few seconds before your death. What would you like to say?"

With a shallow breath, I managed to grunt, "*Go to hell . . .*"

The Megarothke pulled back with his blade and I swear his eyes seemed to smile as the speakers said, "Ah, but we're already here . . ."

PART THREE

Unhappy do I call all those who have only one choice:
either to become evil beasts, or evil beast-tamers. Amongst such would
I not build my tabernacle.
—THUS SPOKE ZARATHUSTRA

22

IN MOTION

HERE WAS A FLASH OF LIGHT; THE MEGAROTHKE'S blade burst into two pieces. Several stories above us, I heard what sounded like a quick succession of controlled blasts, each one closer than the last. Another solid bolt of light pierced through the wall, the briefest, brightest flicker of a laser. This one took off the Megarothke's left lower arm just below the elbow.

With a howl of anguish, the Megarothke backed through the turnstile, and as he did, the cagework fell in hot molten strips around him. To see such a creature flee was a glimpse behind the veil. The immortal became a trick of science in a single burst of light. By the time I'd caught myself on the pavement landing, the Megarothke had gone through the door and into the superstructure.

Within moments of his departure, several teams came around the bend in the steps carrying heavy weaponry. As they rushed by in their trenchcoats, they hardly even looked at me; I didn't recognize a single person until Sarek rounded the corner.

Instead of immediately following on into the structure

like the others, Sarek knelt at the top of the steps, pulled a matte-black rectangular headset down over his eyes, and then peered into the scope of a massive sniper rifle. A Japanese light-cannon—a *Katana*. The gun glimmered with shaved metal and circuit boards like a piece of debris from a spaceship.

From my position down on the landing, I watched Sarek stare through the walls—augmented by the scope and the head set—and slowly adjust his aim like a hunter tracking the path of a distant predator.

With another whip-like crack, a beam of light burst from the barrel of the rifle and sliced through the wall, transpiercing into the open room beyond the gate and God only knows how far beyond. While it was only a momentary flicker, the stream burned into my vision and flickered inverted greens and purples as I blinked and looked away.

While I had no way of knowing if he'd hit his target, or if he was even aiming at the Megarothke, the shot seemed to satisfy him for the moment. Sarek shouldered the weapon and disappeared through the melted metal turnstile and into the open door.

Taking a deep breath and trying to grasp the full scope of the assault, it wasn't until Aria arrived that I felt like things began to make sense. Ectomorphic Aria, with her greasy hair and painfully oversized trench coat, the heartless dispatcher who tasted like cigarette smoke and tears.

I needed her—her presence, her voice, if nothing else.

"Theo," she said, sprinting and practically stumbling down the stairs to slide into place next to me. Voice shaking with emotion. "Theo, Theo, *Theo*—what part of '*don't go down the hole*' did you not understand?"

"Your voice—saved me," I said weakly. Blood had begun to seep through my coat again, creeping past the withering dermapatch solution.

"You've been shot!" she said grabbing my good shoulder and digging with her fingers as she bent in to take a closer look. Then, with furious gestures, she swiped down and examined the rest of my body for wounds, clutching at seams, ripping apart buttons. "I wanted you to be able to hang back and come with my team, or at the very least pull rear security—not die on the front lines like some *fool.*"

"I saw the Megarothke," I said. "I saw him before the war ever began—and I did *nothing.*"

"Stop talking! God, I *hate* you," she said. Leaning in, she grabbed the trench coat and undid all the buttons and central zipper. "I've got some medical supplies. More teams are on the way. Santa Monica sent patrols down all over the city. This is it, Theo. *The* invasion. The Orbital has descended *en masse.* All their soldiers, all their tech, all their research. They say that Los Angeles is going to be the point of rebirth for all of humanity. But what's that going to matter if you *die* down here?"

I nodded and grimaced as she yanked open the trench coat to get a better view of the wound, tearing my undershirt along the ripped sections.

"Easy now, I've been shot," I said through gritted teeth.

"Don't I know it," she said, ripping off a final section of my bloodied shirt so that the wound was clear. "I tried my absolute fucking hardest to warn you in the clearest possible way—at least based on what I knew at the time."

"I thought you were just sleep talking," I lied.

"They wouldn't tell me the full plan until right before we descended—our forces were thick with the Recluse's spies. As far as we know, even our implants were bugged." The communications team followed her, lugging down black crates of equipment to be hastily set in place. Stillson was among them, face blotchy and red. Seeing my face, he broke ranks and approached, but Aria turned and ordered him back to assist the communications team.

"Stillson's alive," I said, a small point of light coming through the clouds. "What about Wensel?"

"One second, Theo, I'm trying to fucking keep you from dying, okay?" Aria said, delicately extracting the mottled, hardened core of dermapatch solution from my chest. All blood drained from her face before she said, "Theo, you should be bleeding a lot more . . ."

"What do you mean?" I asked.

Aria leaned in close now, with the tenderness of a wet nurse, using a disinfectant pad to clean the area where I'd been hit by Krenel's sniper round. "Look," she said, helping guide my head appropriately.

A fist sized patch of skin had been stripped away. Instead of broken rib bones, there was a punctured fibrous of mesh metallic strands. Individual ribs appeared to rise and fall under the skin, but instead of separate bones, the doctors had implanted a collapsible system of carbon fiber bars connected by a composite fabric.

"Oh Jesus . . . you're like a cyborg," Aria said.

"Ah fuck," I said. Maybe not profound, but then, I was staring into my own chest cavity.

"It's okay," Aria said, hand on the side of my face, "We're all technically cyborgs, with our implants—you've just taken it to the next level a bit."

Two medics with sleek black flight suits and blue crosses came down the steps toward us, their chests adorned with Russian and Japanese characters. I was half-way through explaining what happened to Takatoshi and how I'd fought with Junkhead and Krenel when Aria grabbed my chin and looked me in the eyes.

"You're coming with us," she said. "It's not safe to head back up yet. Whole sections have been detonated, and for all I know we're trapped right now."

I nodded.

As the medics helped me to my feet, Aria lead the way to where the communications team had set up a temporary outpost. Rapid fire reports and status updates flowed in a constant stream of overlapping microphone clicks and static. Stillson limped over, a bandage on his leg stained deep red, and updated her as expeditiously as he could. All parties seemed to know that their very lives depended on their competence and focus. Aria nodded and told him to send a report up to Clark.

"We need you to lay flat now," the medic said in a thick Russian accent. The skin on his face looked as if it had been grafted from other parts of his body—or at least from some-*body*. Unzipping a bag at his side, he took out a networked helmet and put it on with the visor still up. "We are from Orbital. This may frighten."

I looked at Aria. She nodded.

I watched the medic's black goggles scan my chest as he slipped his massive hands into light-up gloves and raised an elastic face guard. The second medic, an Asian, knelt next to him, ready to assist.

"Whatever you do—don't move," the Russian medic said, rolling an open crate over to my side.

Then, the Asian medic withdrew a reddish-brown torso-sized octopus and placed it over my chest. The weight and warmth alone made my body seize with terror. The "mouth" instinctively shifted over to the wound, while the "legs" latched around my ribcage and neck with a sickening wet suction sound.

The Russian medic slipped down the visor of his helmet and snapped his light-gloves into action while the Asian medic grabbed the octopus by the head and shoved his hand into a deep cut in the skin. Then, withdrawing three spongy tubes, he began attaching them to various chemical bags.

"Don't worry," the Russian's muffled voice said from within his networked helmet, "This not *real* Octopus. This *Doctor* Octopus . . ."

To my horror, I think he may have been laughing, but between the strange way he conducted his light-up gloves and the immediate sensation of tiny scalpels and tendrils inserting into my chest, I couldn't spare the brain space to try and get the joke.

The radios clicked and pinged in the background, along with the intermittent sound of machine gun fire and explosions. Aria glanced over her shoulders and then back down at me. I balled my fists and promised myself I would never eat seafood again.

"We know this can be a little disconcerting," the Japanese medic said, leaning in close that I could see the reflection of the squirming octopus in his goggles, "but trust me, we are both neuro-augmented specialists, and we never would have made it onto the Orbital if we were bad at our profession."

"I need to brief him whenever it's safe," Aria said, coming around to the far side.

"Proceed," the Russian said, rolling his 'r.'

I stared at the dimly lit drop ceiling above me, the octopus warm on my chest, and searched for Aria. She arrived on the right side, kneeling down and leaning over.

"Officer Abrams," she said, her voice attempting a tone more professional than she could successfully manage at this point, "We don't have much time. Sarek and his teams have surrounded the Megarothke in some sort of cube at the center of a dome. The physics are rough, and they need our intel for battle mapping. In any case, right now they're involved in a protracted battle with a horde of mantises and bruisers along the outer edges. A whole host seems to have rushed up to defend the Megarothke. The bottom line is that in the next five minutes or so, we are going to shift forward to run analysis for them, or retreat to draw a defense line."

I nodded, not sure where I fit in all of this. Looking up at the concern in Aria's eyes, I suddenly realized that I didn't deserve any sort of brief—Aria was firmly in charge of the battlespace reconnaissance, and I was almost completely useless at this point. Which meant that Aria just wanted an excuse to be *near* me. To watch over my surgery.

The thought that she might actually care beyond the limited utility of our surface arrangement almost scared me more than the creature aggressively clutching at my chest. Of course, I knew I loved her, but I was afraid to lose her. I didn't want us to care so openly. To name it, to address it, was to almost certainly lose it. No one I loved survived. That was just how it worked.

"Listen, you have to believe that I wanted to protect you. I was never trying to get you or Takatoshi killed. You were never sacrifices. Honestly, the chances of you finding the Megarothke first were about one and eighty, and even then, I didn't want to risk it.

"Lots of people found huddlers or caches of spider-bots. Lots of people got killed by mantises along the way. But no one in all forty-odd square miles of superstructure went straight to the source like you managed. You and Takatoshi will go down in history as heroes."

I thought about it. Forty square miles of superstructure. How many theaters full of corpses could fit in that space? How many TV-faced robots and Mantis puppeteers? How many patrol members would end up like the skeleton on the catwalk?

"We're near the end, and I need you to hang on, okay? You're not going to do anymore fighting. You just have to survive."

"Officer Aria," the Russians muffled voice said, "The

patient has Phoenix-15 heart—on right side. Cluster sac lungs and muscles all biomimetic. Biofab-robotics. Blood mixed with nano-replicators for accelerated clotting. This is better than Orbital. All he needs are stitches, glue, and juice."

I tried to keep my breathing stable as the octopus sucked on my open chest wound, probing my insides with its strange invasive antenna. What the hell was he talking about?

"You are healthy now," the Russian medic said. A burning sensation was slowly sealing over the wound. "We need fighter. Not patient. Strap the juice packs. Give Dextro. Put gun back in hand."

The Japanese doctor nodded and brought me to a sitting position. Healthy seemed like a wild exaggeration but I wasn't in a stable enough mindset to debate. The octopus slowly detached its tentacles and fell into my arms like a fat, tired puppy. The wound felt like a loaf of warm bread—numb to the touch and freshly sealed. The skin on my chest was steaming from where it had been soldered shut except for a little tube attachment where three hoses could be attached.

The Japanese doctor held the attachment up and said, "Drainage, input, auxiliary." Then slung a backpack around my good shoulder and tightened it across my torso so it sat below the wound. As he connected booster tubes to the attachment, he said, "PRP and Plasma Boosters. These will administer as needed. Lastly, this little clicker right here—we call it nitro. Don't touch it. This should only be used by someone else in the event that your heart stops. If you activate it, you'll be on a downhill rollercoaster for about thirty seconds and then slam straight into the ground."

"I just finished an AR/Ch kit a few hours ago," I said.

"AR/Ch kits are for cavemen," he said. "I worked on Phoenix 15s like yours at Stanford and then brought the procedures to Tokyo. Your heart was manufactured at UCLA, so the surgery had to have been overseen by someone from Geffen. You will be better off than us when the juice packs finish."

"We're moving," Aria called over from the communications center.

We certainly were.

23

PERIMETER

THE DEXTRO THEY'D PUMPED INTO MY BLOOD HAD LEFT me hyper-alert and capable of walking on my own. The dome where they had trapped the Megarothke was about a mile away from our position. We moved tactically, with the valuable and the vulnerable members at the center. I was fairly certain that I was among the latter, and I knew that I wouldn't feel comfortable until I was back up front.

The corridor through the lab was a wide but circuitous route, so we didn't make our ETA. By the time we made it to the edge of the perimeter, the gunmen along the battlements were haggard and bloody. A small detachment had pulled back the wounded from the line and were administering battlefield treatment.

Among the wounded and dead were patrolmen, soldiers, and even civilians: gray trench coats and blue armbands; sleek black flight suits with Orbital goggles; simple jeans, work boots and jackets. The weapons ranged from Katana light-cannons to wood paneled deer hunting rifles. The wounds ranged from deep gashes and punctures to charred, severed limbs.

"Set up against that far wall," Aria said to Stillson. "Make sure that we're safe from any shrapnel that might come over the edge, as well. You there—guide me to the safest vantage point. I want eyes on before we calibrate the systems."

I followed them to the base of the rubble and carefully climbed fifteen feet or so until I could see into the center.

Imagine an indoor stadium where the seating and risers have been reduced to rubble. These leftover piles formed a loose circular barricade, surrounding the central area.

Above us stood a massive dome—a hanger for Orbital tech, or possibly a blast pit. All I knew is that it was far bigger than anything I'd ever conceived could exist underground. Structurally embedded lights shined up from the edges into the expanse above, illuminating lines along the concrete curves which joined at the center like the inside of a globe. At various points these lines were overtaken by charred burns or outbreaks of ash colored mold. The vaulted space was given further form by lingering arcs of tracer smoke, which hung suspended in the emptiness like ghosts of spent fireworks.

Directly under the highest point of the dome sat the obsidian-black cube. The surfaces shifted in a mercurial fashion, like some sort of convection currents pulsed through them without sacrificing the extreme sharpness of the corners and edges.

Surrounding the cube were hundreds of mantis corpses twitching with green blood coating their dark brown carapace. Fiends had been chopped down as well, their crisped patches of fur and claw still festering like road kill. Stray spider-bots crept out of holes, crouching and either healing or feeding on the wounded.

The rotten smell of burnt flesh, gunpowder, and ozone permeated the air with such a pungent odor that it made my face contort. Radios flickered and clicked. Snipers from around the edges took carefully approved shots, picking off spider-bots like target practice.

Even from my limited perspective, with my limited knowledge, the situation was clear to me: we had no idea what we'd found. Pushing up gently with my right arm and then descending from the barricade, I returned to the communications station.

Aria was carefully managing the set-up process. Several workers were placing satellite dishes and antennas on extended poles which were strapped to the desks. Two holographic projectors had been coordinated, and in front of the desks, a miniature three-dimensional feed of our situation was in the process of creation. At the center of the holographic field sat the cube—impenetrable and obscene—even with the ultra-complexity of heat signatures, EMR readings, and structural analysis rippling across the software, the cube was a wall of solid purple.

I asked one of the techs for permission to access the battlefield in my implants. After looking to Aria for approval, he acceded. A simplified version of the purple cube with a green ring around it appeared as a transparent overlay in the lower left hand corner of my vision field. There must have been at least a hundred fighters along the barricade, blue outlines shifting and stretching.

In my head, I did some quick estimates: the cube was one hundred yards in, that made the diameter two hundred. That times pi had to be around what? A little under six hundred and fifty? So there should have been a person per every six or seven yards, but I could see that they were clumped up in some areas and spread woefully thin in others. The wall in front of us barely had three or four soldiers within shouting distance.

Stillson looked up at me from one of the desks and must have noticed what I was doing.

"Theo, I can't tell you how good it is to see you alive," he said, approaching me with a rifle in hand.

"Likewise," I said, feeling a sudden rush of nostalgia for our patrol squad.

"You're wounded, but can you still shoot?"

"Of course," I said.

"Alright then," he said, handing me a Katana light-cannon covered in blood. "I'm not asking you to take a spot on the barricade, but I don't want to see you stranded with nothing but a pistol if the next wave overwhelms the perimeter."

The stock was shaved aluminum; it smelled like battery acid. Kanji was emblazoned along the sides of the square barrel like a true samurai sword.

"It'd be an honor. There's a thirty yard gap at about nine o'clock on the map," I said. We were currently standing at about six o'clock. My words came automatically at this point. Thoughts came automatically. The delayed onset of the dextro was still cranking like an organ grinder in my brain.

"Theo, take a spot right there where I can see you," Aria said from her spot at the communications desks, pointing to a notch in the barricade about ten yards away. I could tell she was trying to appear as impartial as possible, but her voice faltered, "You're still wounded—" She tried to continue, but there were no words. We simply looked at each other.

Stillson looked at me and then back at her.

"Received," I said. "You can count on me. I'll hold my ground."

Aria nodded and glanced nervously back at the holographic field and then back at us.

"We're all about to die here," Stillson said. "I think you can drop the act."

I smiled. Aria appeared not to have heard him. She'd already dived back into managing the rest of the technicians.

Stillson clipped a radio to my collar, as well. "We'd use our implants for orders, but about fifty percent of the force down here are civilians and couldn't get the surgery in time. From the images and updates we were getting along the way, it seems a lot of them can barely fire their rifle. You think you have a shot at something dangerous, aim low and fire. But if you just want to pick off spider-bots, call it in."

"Roger," I said, cradling the rifle in my right arm and eyeing the spot I was about to take.

"You want a smoke?" Stillson asked.

"Won't that give away my position?"

"It might," he said. "But we need sanity more than cover. There's been some strange shit coming out of that cube. It's your call."

I thought about the TV-faced robot, the theater, and the corpse marionettes. "Yeah, fuck it. I'll take a smoke."

Stillson, noticing my right arm was holding the rifle and my left wounded, stepped forward and put the cigarette in my lips like a boxing coach giving water to a prizefighter. Then he lit it, patted me on the back, and said, "Don't get killed, son."

I nodded at him and then winked at Aria, who was watching us again over her shoulder. I took my spot on the barricade.

From my notch, I could see the scopes and pale faces of soldiers across the way. The radio snapped in and out, receiving updates and keeping people calm. Every few minutes, communications would grant a shot and a spider-bot would burst into clouds of circuitry and battery acid.

Holding the cigarette delicately between my teeth, my eyes followed a steel chain that dipped out over the chunks of concrete and then began again down below, with a large iron hook lying on a bed of vinyl canvas. The chain looked light enough to swing but heavy enough to do serious damage.

I tucked the thought away in the back of my mind as I peered into the scope of the light cannon and studied the corpses of the Scourge. Among the punctured carapace of the mantises, there were modified body parts—limbs that ended in curved blades and what appeared to be snub-nosed laser cannons. The Megarothke had clearly bestowed them with a certain amount of science.

I took a long, slow drag off the cigarette, which was around halfway finished. All quiet on the subterranean front, I thought to myself. The cube was resolute; a mockery to our anxious anticipation. I let out the smoke through the left side of my mouth and tried to think of what it might hold. About whether or not it was a portal of sorts. The holograph showed no signs of tunnels or trap doors immediately beneath it. There were no escape routes or elevators to deeper levels.

Radio chatter picked up as the situation calmed down. Disaffected voices casting doubts on the strategy. Others claiming they didn't even know we had a strategy. A vaguely Russian voice kept telling people to shut up because they were blocking valuable space on the channel, but ironically he kept getting cut off before he could deliver the message.

"Who are these Russian guys anyway?" one voice said. "And since when did they get to tell us what to do?"

I cringed.

"I'm a goddamn American, that's all I know, and we survived this long without getting sent down a giant hole to stare at some cube," another said.

"How do we know we aren't being used by the Orbital?"

"Aren't they all cyborgs anyway?"

I took another deep drag, leaning into my rifle and waiting for some form of authority to take charge.

"Good morning," a voice rippled through our radios like

a dark current. The depth and power of the voice silenced all other chatter.

My heart nearly stopped. The radios stayed silent. I knew the voice.

The Megarothke was ready to address his audience.

24

***THE HOLLOW WAR
02/02/2044

B Y THE TIME THE SUN CAME UP, EVERY MAJOR CITY IN the world—except Los Angeles—had been bombed to the ground. Death counts and doomsday prophets cluttered the radio stations that were left, but the only thing truly important to me was finding Amelie.

Weaving through the freeway traffic jam on a stolen motorcycle, I made my way toward Phillon's house on the hill. The gate was broken, so I had to try to manually pry it open. When that failed, I left the bike, scaled the fence, and jogged up the driveway as fast as I could.

Ohara had been trying to reach me all morning, trying to help organize his section of the LAPD, but family came first. The sliding glass doors were disabled, and since there weren't any handles, I was forced to try to kick them in. Except the panels were ballistic glass, so after a few kicks which did nothing but leave scuff marks, I took out my gun and I shot the locking mechanism. The track-lining was jammed, but I was able to pull it far enough back to where I could slip through.

The house was incredibly warm—like a dry sauna—but

even worse was the quiet. The world outside was composed of smoke, screams and sirens, and yet inside the glass it felt like a tomb buried deep within a pyramid.

No one was in the living room, and there was no sign of any disturbance, either. Three white couches, a coffee table, a television covering most of the far wall. I continued, heading down the hallway, venturing farther into the house than I'd ever gone. Clarence had mentioned something about building an astral-lab below, but I hadn't seen any of them since the séance almost three weeks earlier.

After the meeting, we'd all flown back from the bed and breakfast together. Jack Batch had stared out the window most of the way, sitting perfectly still and offering no conversation whatsoever. No real crime had been perpetrated. No one at the station would have believed a person could be "possessed" by a "hybrid."

Even still, I had watched him, aware that some sort of dark change had occurred.

Calling down the hallway, I waited to hear if anyone would respond, but the house seemed to swallow my voice. The bathroom door had been left open, an exercise room was empty down toward one end of the hall, and the master bedroom was empty, as well—if not exactly clean. In fact, it looked as if someone had ransacked the dressers and closet. Perhaps in flight.

But would they have gone? Where could be more safe than here?

There was one last doorway in the hall, one that had been added recently. Bits of plaster still lay on the ground, and someone had neglected to remove the protective tape when they finished staining the wooden frame. After knocking loudly, I opened the door and found myself at the top of a steep, winding staircase.

If they were here, they would be down below.

"Hey, I'm coming down," I called out. "It's Theo, so don't shoot me or anything."

I waited, but there was no response. The only sound was a low hum, which would rise and fall with a wavering consistency. Despite being made of grated metal, the stair seemed to bend and flex under my feet. I thought about drawing my weapon but then decided against it. There was enough panic above.

After spiraling down two or three levels, the staircase ended at a large room with seven or eight empty VR Coffins. These were the next wave in VR tech. The coffins were where you went to "die" while deep diving on the other side. Medical hooks ups and scans monitored your health, allowing you to stay under for days if needed.

The room was dim, lit by several emergency LED strips along the ceiling. Upon entering, an odd, tingling sensation crawled under my skin, and when I looked down at my arm, all of my hair was standing on end. Among the various devices situated within the lab, errant bits of static electricity lit and sparked.

A stench of iron, ozone, and shaved metal hung within the stagnant atmosphere, and several bodies lay on the ground in the center of the coffin circle. All adults.

The first was Clarence, lying face up, with several stab wounds through the center of his chest and a deep, clean slash that had cleft his facial structure without actually crushing or displacing any of his features. The type of cut a samurai blade might leave.

The second was Phillon, body curled, into a loose fetal position, a thick slime of blood hanging from his lips. I bent down and looked at his eyes, which were still open, staring into the plane of the afterlife. I thought about closing them, but I knew more than anything, I had to face the third body first.

Mathew lay face down, arms up. Gently shaking his shoulder, there was a secret, desperate part of me that thought he might shrug and roll over. That he might make some smart remark in a groggy voice and slap away my hand. But instead, his shoulder felt stiff, devoid of any remaining human warmth.

Slowly reaching down, I turned him over to inspect the damage. I now recognized that whereas the others had been merely killed, Mathew had been . . . well, I couldn't exactly be sure. One of his arms had been removed at the elbow, and lay several feet away. Both his shirt and pants had been slit and peeled back, and one of his breasts had been bisected, like some lab specimen. It didn't stop there, though. Below the rib cage, his entire stomach had been worked upon, jumbled around, with the intestines and the ovaries, all the way down to the genitalia.

Whatever had done this had been curious and cruel in the most clinical of senses. I felt numb; I felt nothing. A part of me detached and stared down at the situation with the cold lens of the perpetrator—neither scientist nor sadist— something else entirely.

There was a part of me that believed I had never truly *felt*, and would never feel again. That the world had always been an endless series of lists and scrolls, my consciousness an entombed, impenetrable archive of unencumbered data.

That was what scared me. The realization that I was not shocked. That I had expected this and accepted it long before I'd ever even known it was possible. That I had secretly wanted it. That I considered obliteration the only true form of peace.

Taking a step back, I shook my head and took a deep breath. Walking to the corner of the room, where some blankets and supplies had been stored, I grabbed one of the blankets and the brought it back to spread over Mathew's body.

I had to ground myself within the practical: the question

at hand was whether I should look to see if Amelie might have hidden away somewhere, or immediately try to locate Frau Kershner at the Montessori school in Long Beach.

Then, looking at the arrangement of the VR coffins, I noticed there was a dark black circle in the center of them, shaped almost like a manhole. Crouching down, I wiped the dark blotch with my finger and found that the tile within it had been turned into a soft, delicate ash. Still crouching, I rubbed the soft ash between my fingers when voice came from behind me.

"Theo," the voice said.

It was Phillon. I spun and looked at him. His eyes hadn't moved, but the thick dredge of slime had broken from his lips.

"There is no God, Theo," Phillon said, voice no more than a faint, barely enunciated whisper. "I was a fraud . . . In the end, I was just another fraud . . ."

Stepping over to him and bending down in front of his face to hear better, I tried to see if his eyes might register some last flicker of humanity.

"Phillon," I asked. "Phillon, what happened here? Who did this?"

Phillon stared at the ground in front of him.

"Phillon, where's Amelie?"

"Gone . . ." Phillon said. Or rather, the sound simply seemed to have emanated from his throat from some other-worldly spirit.

"Phillon, don't worry, we'll get someone down here to help you, okay?"

"The sin of man . . ." his voice said.

I waited, saying nothing. I knew these were his last words.

"Came to wipe away, the sin of man . . ."

And with that, the light went out of his eyes.

25

***DOUBLE-BARREL

O HARA WAS IN A LARGE COMMAND ROOM FULL OF cops and soldiers, pouring over an ancient, wall-mounted map with blinking LEDs that showed the status of power plants and communication towers throughout Southern California. Outside Joint Base Los Alamitos, a crowd around five thousand strong had gathered in front of the main gates. I was still sweating from the ride, having been guided around the back of the base to a tunnel entrance under a warehouse.

"Theo," Ohara said when he saw me. "Have you seen anyone else from our squad?"

"No," I said. "What's the plan here?"

"Fuck if I know," Ohara said. On one side of the room, a group of officers were stocking rifle magazines with quick-loaders. The sound of metal-on-metal scraped with a mechanical rapidity that raised the overall volume in the room two-fold. "This is the only base in the country that wasn't bombed from the inside. We're just trying to hold the perimeter until we can make contact with someone."

"And what if there's no one left?" I asked.

I'd stopped by Amelie's Montessori school only to find it abandoned. Frau Kershner's home had been looted and covered in anti-Semitic graffiti. The phones were offline and all non-EMS servers seemed to have been either destroyed or indefinitely suspended.

"Then we're fucked," Ohara said.

"Listen, remember that guy, Jack Batch?" I asked.

Ohara stared at me, as if trying to focus through the noise.

"Follow me," I said, grabbing his arm and leading him into the hallway. From the second story window we could see the crowd gathered outside. A girl had climbed up on the fence and was leading some sort of chant.

"Remember how Mathew started dating that guy, and they formed a sort of cult and it all culminated that weird séance? Remember how I told you about it over drinks, how I needed your support in keeping Amelie away from all of them? The restraining order we were gonna seek?"

Ohara nodded, "Yeah, I do. Sure."

"While we were there, they made contact with this creature called the Lightbringer, and they said it was going to bring about some new world. They said he was the most powerful hybrid on the planet right now, and that he was controlling all of the other A.I. entities. Anyway, one of the guys at the séance was Jack Batch, co-founder of Haverston-Batch."

"Okay . . ."

"Right now," I said, looking down and then looking back up at him, "We are currently standing over the largest Haverston-Batch laboratory in the world. All of their top R&D was classified and kept down in the vaults."

Ohara looked at me, the chanting outside growing louder and ever more indiscernible.

"At the séance, Jack Batch allowed the Lightbringer to go inside him, to take control of him, and then he said—he *literally* said, 'I know where the Lightbringer's body is—I need to go visit one of my labs, the one in Los Alamitos.'"

Ohara wiped his forehead and looked down at his shoes. "Listen Theo, I know this is all crystal clear to you, but I'm going to need you to like—*tell me what the fuck you are try-ing to say.* I feel like I'm missing a lot of critical stuff here."

I shook my head and tried to focus with my hands in front of me: "Jack Batch came back to Los Alamitos to set free a creature called the Lightbringer. That creature must have triggered the bombs that initiated all of this horror—it's the only way any of it makes sense. I'm not a crazy per-son, Ohara, I've just—I didn't think he would *actually* try to bring about the apocalypse. But doesn't it seem a lit-tle suspicious that this is the only military base that wasn't destroyed?"

Ohara stared at me. I felt like I was making a solid case, but from his point of view, this was mostly brand new infor-mation. I probably looked like a sweaty, paranoid mess.

"What proof could you actually have? This could be the Russians for all we know," Ohara said. "Where's Mathew? What's he think about all this?"

"Mathew's dead," I said, losing patience, and then real-izing that I had completely blocked out the incident. The images of their bloodied corpses poured down onto my brain like loose stacks falling from a closet, and I had to bring my hands up to my forehead and squeeze to be able to focus and press through. "I found him, Phillon and Clarence all stabbed to death back at the astral lab they'd built under their house. Jack Batch is the only one missing, and I'm pretty sure he's here, right now, down in the vaults."

"So what should we do?"

"We should try to see if we can find some way to breach the security," I said. "Before it's too late." And with that, I started walking down the hall. There had been a component of heavily armed Special Forces members around the entrance to the SCIF located at the center of the base.

Ohara hurried to follow, calling out that I was acting like a lunatic, but when I turned the corner, I found myself standing in front of a man in a trucker hat, torn-up boots and blue jeans. Beads of blue sweat had formed across his brow and stained his neck and arm pits, but most concerning of all was the twentieth century, double barrel shot gun held tightly within his grip.

"T'all started here. T'all ends here," the man said in a grizzly smoker's voice.

"Wait," I said, holding up my hands.

But there was no negotiation. The shotgun exploded less than ten feet away, catching me in the chest like a bullet train. I was lifted off my feet and hit the ground solid. There was no pain, only disbelief. Only a flicker of horror that everything had been cut short. The last thing I remember was the second shotgun blast, and seeing Ohara's headless corpse land next to mine, the blood from his open neck gushing into a dark red pool.

26

IMMORTAL
07/07/2051

"THERE IS NO ESCAPE, DEAR HUMANS, FROM YOUR eventual last breath," the Megarothke said through the speakers on our collars. "Whether I bring about your end in the next few minutes, or whether you live a long and pathetic life, scraping along the damaged husk of the Earth, you will eventually die. Your blood is radioactive. Your children will be infertile. The world will forget you ever existed."

Suddenly a massive creature appeared above us, holographic light outlined in the smoke and fog, its legs spanning the entire killing field. It was the Megarothke, projected over us like a pagan god. Screams echoed around the barricade, along with bursts of fire.

"I initiated the Hollow War. I set the beasts loose for the Harvest. I planted the new variations of species all over the world. The fiends to hunt your stragglers. The bruisers to dismantle your cities. The spider-bots, my watchful eyes. I am the end and the beginning of all that you have ever been. Once it was said that man was a bridge, from beast to the Ubermensch. I say, *from beast to the Megarothke.*

"I am the lord of the new creations, which will one day colonize the stars. Even now, they grow within the deep pockets of the Earth, waiting to be born. Your place is now fixed, forever to remain a simple rung in the ladder of our evolution.

"Know this, humans," the Megarothke stated, his holograph swinging his broadsword in a slow, sweeping motion across the barricades, its ghostly light trailing in the plumes of smoke. "You crept forth in the night like an adder and bit at me. You think that your poison is fatal, but I ask of you: *When has a dragon ever died from the poison of a snake?*

"I tell you: *Take back your poison—you are not rich enough to give it to me.*

"I spare you now not out of mercy, but out of respect for the power that your reintegrated sentience could wield within the Earth Reborn. The Orbital is a false god. Your old religions were full of false gods. Your slave morality is a false god. Cast it aside. Only transvaluation will save you. Immortality is within your reach. Eternal life. But you will not find it in human form.

"Consider your leadership, so ready to sacrifice you. To throw you to certain death. Consider Santa Monica, who fed you to me each month like chattel. Though your leaders did not know it, those that were sacrificed were also saved, by my hand, as you may be. Consider the Orbital, a vector of the worst disease known to man. A ship of blind vampires waiting to swoop down upon you. They will devour you one piece at a time. They are not your equals. They are not leaders; they are predators.

"For too long I have watched as the last bits and pieces of humanity clung to this Earth. The time for you to leave your physical bodies has arrived. Now is when you must make your final choice: eternity or oblivion. I will not allow you to stand in the way any longer. I have offered you the best, most assured salvation that any creature has ever proffered in the history of the universe.

"If you will join me, stand now and enter the cube."

•

There was a slow inhalation, a moment of strange, terrible consideration, before finally the silence was broken. With a simple click, the radios turned back on and the image of the creature disappeared. The center of the dome was once more a swirl of darkened smoke.

"Those were lies," the Sarek's voice said over the comms. "We've had our own spy operations—the Megarothke is afraid of the Orbital—afraid of Los Angeles. The Megarothke is not God, he is only flesh and blood. We do not need a miracle to defeat him, only our courage and a will to fight. Now is our one chance to stand and reclaim our rightful place."

"Bullshit!"

"What just—"

"Nobody—"

"We can't—"

The radio discipline of our perimeter was a nightmare. I looked at the cigarette, which had long died in my fingers. After giving it a few puffs to see if there was any flame left, I flicked it out over the barricade. No one had entered the killing field yet, but one man was standing on top of the barricade to my left. If I was six o'clock in the perimeter, he would have been at around nine.

"Listen to my words," Sarek's voice cut in through the radio chatter, overriding all other voices. "I know some of you are untrained, but there are no civilians here. We are all soldiers now. If anyone, *anyone*, crosses the barricade, I will personally restore order with my light cannon."

"So you're going to shoot—"

"You're just going to kill us—"

"A guy next to me got his head eaten off—"

"—if we don't follow your suicide mission?"

The same choir of discordant voices rose back up, cutting each other off and interrupting each sentence before could even properly begin, until all of the sudden the radios went silent.

"I will send you a comforter," the Megarothke said.

I waited for the radios to turn back on, but they stayed eerily silent. Behind me, the techs yelled back and forth, trying to reboot their systems, while Aria repeatedly called in signal strength tests to Sarek and someone named Rachmanivich.

Then the lights went out and darkness fell over us like a thick black cape.

Until then, I hadn't fully appreciated the light. Looking over my shoulder at the edges of the dome, I realized I had taken it completely for granted that the dome was lit when I arrived. Perhaps I had put too much faith in the Orbital, believing that it had been produced by one of their undeclared inventions.

With the radios out, people shouted back and forth to each other like shipwrecked sailors in the night. As soon as my implants adjusted, I could make out the edges of the space again, the dome looming above us, but the far side of the perimeter was nothing but a faint blur. Flashlights flicked on and casted about, but what caught my attention most was the fact that the edges of the cube had begun to glow with a ghostly light, framing it perfectly within the darkness.

Like raindrops forming on a gutter, torso-sized phosphorescent amoebas of mist began to coalesce on the black, angular surface of the cube. One by one, they split off and hovered over the ground, spinning out in a slow spiral orbit across the killing field. At first there were only two or three, but then five and fifteen, until there were nearly a hundred.

Without radios, there was no debate, only theories lobbed into midair and orders to hold our positions. As the twisting shapes came closer, like ships coursing through an invisible sea, they began to change form, to take on first a wind-blown vertical crescent and then arms and legs— walking slowly.

"Activate the EMP," Aria ordered from behind me.

Another voice sounded as well, and when I looked back over my shoulder, it was none other than Sarek. "*Strui okno beta sem,*" Sarek shouted. "*Aktivirovat* Death-Bringer."

At his command, a pile of the seamless, jet black containers that had been hauled in beforehand began to shift and disassemble. Puffs of frost and steam hissed and groaned as the surfaces of the largest crate formed a platform that opened around a chrome cylinder the size of a pocket-warhead.

"You fire that inside and we're all dead," Aria called out.

"Listen, you didn't even know this cube was down here until we came," Sarek responded. "I'm literally the only one that can save you now."

I wanted to listen, but when I saw what was hovering out in front of me, I felt my worlds schism and slide apart.

It was *Madison*.

Not ten feet away, floating above the rubble.

With dark translucent curls held up in a bun and albescent skin, she wore an evening gown with pendants over her shoulders.

"Bet you never thought you'd see me like this," Madison said.

"You're going to blow the whole dome," I heard Aria say, behind me.

"Trust me, dura," Sarek said caustically. "This will blow a whole lot more than the dome."

I stared in disbelief.

I hadn't seen Madison with long hair in nearly ten years.

"Beyond ourselves, we can be anything. I could be the woman you always wanted me to be."

Madison stared at me as she spoke, gaze dark and focused. I had a tendency to get lost in her eyes. I remembered now, the way she would look up at me, eyes almost closed in the moment of climax. The dress went all the way down to her ankles, with her bare feet pointed at the ground. But the curves within her ghostly fabric left little to the imagination.

"All I ever wanted was to be there for you when you got home, to help you shoulder life's burdens. To share the rainy nights and the sandy vacations and every moment of Amelie's childhood," Madison said. "All I ever wanted was to give you the life we should have had, Theo. The life we promised each other."

"If we fire the EMP, half of our weapons will go offline," Sarek's voice said.

"If we don't fire it, we'll lose half our soldiers outright."

"Our best weapons are more important than our worst soldiers."

I pushed myself up and looked out across the perimeter. With Madison there, it felt easier to stand, as if her presence had infused me with a new, calm energy. Like a current had risen around me, and all I had to do was let go and it would carry me to a place where pain could no longer touch me. Hundreds of ghosts had formed now, delivering the gospel of the Megarothke to each soldier along the notches like minute hands on a clock.

Caught in Madison's hypnotic gaze, a tingling sensation prickled at the back of my throat. Almost like an allergic reaction, as if finely haired vines were trying to push up and out past my uvula. For a moment, I actually gagged, and then to my disbelief, a dream-like substance began to pour from my parted lips.

Holding my left hand out, my skin reflected the silver aura back at me and it gleamed along the barrel of my rifle. The ghostly presence continued to push and grow—the teleplasmic pseudopod worked its way up past my esophagus and uncurled effortlessly from my open mouth. With the slimy tissue of an eel, I could feel it in my throat as it moved in concertina thrusts through the air down into the killing field where Madison stood.

Finally, it planted itself next to Madison with a twisting finish, and burst into a shimmering dust that formed into a perfectly unharmed three-year-old girl.

I nearly collapsed.

I hadn't breathed during the entire process. Shaking at the knees, I looked at the near perfect recreation of Amelie. Or should I say *too* perfect; a recreation from the world of *being.*

Amelie stared up at me. Reaching up and taking her mother's hand, they both stood without judgment or agenda, simply observing my situation. I looked down at the steel chain near my feet. The light of their presence reflected on the links like a path home. I felt wretched, bloodstained, and scuffed. Sweat and dirt coated every crease and pore of my body. One hand nearly useless, the other holding a Japanese light-cannon, which seemed to me now like it never should have been created in the first place.

"Theo, humanity expended all of its most valuable time and energy on two things: violence and self-indulgence. Can't you see that there is more for us on the other side? Can't you see that your decaying husk of a body is the only thing holding back your mind from true happiness?"

"Theo, lay back down in your position or I'll drop you myself," a firm voice said beside me. It was Sarek. Apparently his argument with Aria was over, or at least on hold.

I turned and looked at him, barrel of the light cannon pointed right at my head. Across the killing field where streams of soldiers were following their better-halves and lost relatives toward the cube. I wanted to follow them. I wanted to follow Madison and Amelie home. But I also knew it was a lie, and that the sooner it ended, the better.

"Don't worry about me," I said. "This isn't my family."

Sarek smirked and turned to observe the field like a eighteenth-century general controlling the battle from a nearby hill.

Then he raised the Katana light cannon, took careful aim, and fired.

The skull of a soldier closest to the cube burst like a cherry tomato in a microwave.

"If anyone takes another step closer," Sarek shouted, his voice impossibly loud for a mere human, "I will cut—them—down."

Then as if to make his point clear, he sighted and fired off another round. Another soldier hit the ground.

Sarek fired off another shot. Three down. This got a few soldiers attention, causing them to shake their heads as if they'd snapped out of a trance, but the majority of them continued to step slowly, stumbling across the fiend and mantis remains. In my transparent mini-feed, over half of the blue soldiers had left their position and were headed in.

"Sarek!" Aria's voice sounded. Turning to look at her, I saw her standing within wall of tech soldiers. "We've had enough of your slaughter. We're launching whether you approve or not."

Sarek simply turned and looked at Aria. Multiple soldiers had already entered the cube at this point, bodies glowing for a moment before they disappeared.

"This is our city. These are our men and women," Aria said. "And they deserve a chance."

With a deep bass *oomph* that shook the floor from a machine back near the door, a glowing electric bolus fired deep into the dome. In a crouch, I traced the path up into the sky and then watched as it came down and burst next to the cube in a flash of electric blue.

With a loud crack that echoed off the domed ceiling, a bright blue wave blasted out from the center of the field, taking out all of the flashlights and electronics with it. When I blinked again, Madison and Amelie were nothing but inverted images burned into my eyes.

The cube still stood, eternal as a monolith, illuminated only by a faint, barely perceptible glow.

Once again, we found ourselves in the dark.

27

STICKS AND STONES

HE CUBE HAD BEGUN TO GLOW BRIGHTER AT THE center of the field, pulsing with a rhythmic energy, a paean to whatever dark forces lay within. The rest of the dome was black. Spotty flashlights flickered intermittently—civilians trying to figure out their weapons. One or two beams tried to illuminate the killing field, light tracing up the carnage and before fading into a faint glow.

"All *Kovcheg Soldaty*, the EMP blast has knocked your Katanas offline. Pull back until you've restocked," Sarek's voice said over the radio. "If you need a last-gen weapon, disarm a civilian."

The radio clicked off.

If what Sarek had said was true, the weapon in my hand, the vaunted Katana Light-Cannon, was useless. I had no clue how to repair it and no one had time to explain. Dropping slowly to one knee, I set it down on top of the barricade. As I cleared a spot for it to rest, my hands brushed across the chain. Yanking up on it reflexively, I began to gather the chain in a coil at my feet. The heavy cast-iron hook at the end made a satisfying sound as it dragged up across the broken chunks of concrete and bent metal planks. Eventually, I would have to act. Although I didn't know it at the time, the foundations of my own private assault must have already been laid in my mind.

Checking on the situation behind the line, I watched as Aria maintained her command of the holographic display, guarded by a phalanx of tech officers and patrolmen. For the moment, I couldn't be sure if the real danger lay in the killing fields or at the com station. Sarek had approached the disassembled crate, upon which the chrome capsule revealed the contents with a liquid flourish, like mercury receding. Sarek then withdrew a weapon shaped like a massive red telescope with a padded shoulder-mount.

A Death-Bringer.

A recoilless railgun so powerful it could cause seismic waves strong enough to shift fault lines. To fire that weapon in this room would be suicide. I'd seen videos of a Death-Bringer shot from a helicopter into a mountainside. It was as if God himself had reached down and flattened the trees for nearly a mile. They estimated the shards of the projectile lodged forty-miles deep, penetrating the crust of the Earth.

"You fire that thing in here," Aria said, "And none of us walk out alive. You'll cause an earthquake that will destroy half the clusters in Los Angeles."

Sarek mounted the weapon on his shoulder and turned toward to the group. The tech officers flinched at the sight of the open barrel.

"You think this insertion is about Los Angeles? This is about *humanity*."

"Save it, Sarek. You acted so smart, coming down from your space-station, but now you're here in the middle of the shit-storm and the best you can think of is mass suicide," Aria said. "We've been on the ground for seven years, eking it out. What if it doesn't kill him? What if the Megarothke survives in the cube and the rest of us are dead?"

"Then we lose," Sarek said.

As if on cue, there was a sudden strobing from the cube.

A single voice flowed out from the radios, echoing off the domed roof:

"You should have come when you had the chance," the Megarothke said, voice filling the room like a ghoulish cloud. "At least then you could have died with the memory of your loved ones."

Looking back toward the battlefield, I was temporarily blinded by a flash of light. I blinked and the arachnid form of the Megarothke was burned into the back of my eyes.

The strobe-light set in again: this time centered on a white sphere of light. The edges of the sphere flickered and crackled like loose electricity and the silhouette of the Megarothke within moved in choppy snap-frames across the field.

In two or three strobe-clicks, the Megarothke lifted his blade and thrust it into a dark black patch that appeared to float in front of him. A soldier at three o'clock screamed in pain and went down, flashlight toppling down the barricade. When the sword was pulled back, a curtain of blood spilled from the blade.

In the total darkness of the dome, the Megarothke flickered again, this time in a different location. His sword transpierced into several different dark patches within the sphere. Screams from eight o'clock and eleven o'clock rang out. Sprays of blood came back with each withdrawal.

Then: darkness, coarse shouting, shots fired. I couldn't make heads or tails of it. People were shooting at blind-spots now, vision seared and damaged. As fast as the Megarothke could stab, the sword flickered through the portals like a snake's tongue. Chests and stomachs sloughed loose like sacks of barley bursting at the seams, lit only by the crack-ling brilliance of the strobing energy shield.

Stab-scream-teleport.

The sequence of events happened so quickly that my brain could hardly process it, much less react appropri-ately. The screams were constant now—overlapping cre-scendos. Three more times, the Megarothke appeared and disappeared, each time in a different location, until it seemed that our once airtight perimeter was now a mere constellation.

"Just get the lights up," I heard Aria order from below.

And suddenly, there was light again. The edges of the dome spilt forth illumination, and the Megarothke was crouched like a spider out in the killing fields, hunched down and low-slung. The black scarf was swaddled around the lower half of his face and neck. With a whip-crack, he appeared on the very far side of the barricade, and then over next to us, and then back to the center—each time accompanied by screams and the transparent shell that bris-tled with arcs of electricity.

By a loose estimate, there may have been twenty-five soldiers or less left at this point. Automatic weapons now rang out, spraying the areas where he had been or might soon be, and in the back of my mind, I wondered if this was the end game, and within another thirty seconds there would be no one left at all.

But then, for some reason, the Megarothke stood his ground. Positioned in the center, near the cube, he faced us. I wanted to make some sort of stand, but it was clear that shooting from a distance wasn't working and I wasn't sure what could possibly be effective. Someone needed to get closer. Someone needed to get right up in his face.

Bullets rained down upon the sphere of white energy like rain on an umbrella. The Megarothke barely seemed to notice or care. The hot lead crackled and buzzed as it sprayed out at odd angles. Instead, the Megarothke was looking at Sarek, who stood holding the Death-Bringer.

"When I finish with you," the Megarothke's voice said through the speakers, "I'm coming straight for the Orbital."

"*Na svyazi,*" Sarek said.

Then the railgun lurched on his shoulder, rocking back ever so slightly. A bluish glow flashed from the barrel, but instead of an explosion, it sounded like someone took a crowbar to the inside of a grand piano. A short, stunted, tonal peal.

Before I could even fully register what had happened, Sarek stood with a three-foot metal projectile jutting through his chest and out his back. The Megarothke stood his ground in the center of the field, two black patches burned into the crackling white shell. A stream of tightly knit contrails traced the rail gun projectiles path, entering and exiting the shrinking patches. It was as if the Megarothke had opened the fabric of space and flung the projectile back at Sarek. For all I knew, that pointed steel rod could have traveled a hundred miles within another dimension.

Sarek dropped to his knees, and then fell face down, the bloodied spike facing up like a vicious territorial claim. The Death-Bringer rolled disgracefully down the barricade, smoking from both ends, to join the rubble at the edge of the killing field.

Shit, I thought to myself.

All across the perimeter, shots cracked the silence, but now instead of ignoring them, the Megarothke seemed to twitch, as if he were being pelted or stung—spots of dark blue blood trickled down his skin. From his stable spot, using the broadsword that had been split in half by Sarek's light cannon back on the staircase, the Megarothke continued to stab into the portals with measured articulation.

Frozen in speculation and awe, it wasn't until I heard a woman's scream behind me that I knew I had to act. Looking back at Aria, I saw her drop to her knees as several tech officers rushed to her side. A torrent of blood gushed from the loose fabric of her trench coat around the stomach.

There was no going back now.

This was it.

Springing up from my kneeling position, I dragged the chain behind me as I raced down from the barricade into the killing field. The world seemed to fade a deeper crimson with each step. Shots continued to ring out, striking the Megarothke in the sides, which is perhaps why he didn't seem to have registered me as a threat. Picking up steam, using my one good arm, I swung the thin chain in a wide arch. The centrifugal force of the hook shook my entire body as it orbited, carrying me forward with each lunge. By the time the Megarothke even looked up to address me, I was less than twenty yards away.

Like film-splice cigarette burns, black patches appeared in front of me. I shifted instinctively, twisting my body to avoid the Megarothke's blade as it shot through the portals. Ten yards. The hook was the wrong end of the orbit though, so I pivoted and ran diagonal, hoping I might avoid the next round of blades.

The chain swung around now, and as I looked up at the Megarothke, I could see that he was actually juggling the volley of fire coming at him within linked portals. Forty or fifty different pairs of intermingled dimensional tears, passing bullets like schools of fish until they could be dropped at his side or flung back out into space. One of his arms had been shot off and the other held the blade, but his other two free hands directed the timing and pitch of the portals like an orchestra conductor.

The heavy hook arched, pulling me forward with it, and when it was just about to collide with the Megarothke's head, he opened up a portal to catch it.

I grunted as the chain jerked and the hook disappeared within it. But then another dark patch appeared on the other side of the Megarothke and the hook slammed through it—still carrying with it a deadly arc—which jerked and wrapped back around at the Megarothke's head a second time, catching him in the temple.

With a crack, all the portals disappeared and the chain wrapped itself around his neck and torso. Hundreds of bullets sprayed out from the spots around like a grenade. With a heave, I tightened my core and pulled on the chain in the direction of the cube.

The black sheen that had looked so solid from afar now looked like a smooth current of crude oil, a dark curtain into the unknown. With all of the power left inside me, holding the chain as tightly as I could, I pushed into the fold.

28

ZOOPHAGE

LIKE DIVING INTO A POOL, BUT FINDING ONLY ZERO gravity. There was a definite sensation of breaking through the surface of the cube, and my momentum was more than halved, but rather than falling, I found myself floating downward through a transparent crystalline blue. Reaching out, my arms could feel that the space contained a substance—a force, a thickness—but my fingers felt nothing. They merely grasped at weightlessness. Below me sat an aqua-marine surface, and at my sides, transparent walls that appeared to lead to a great antechamber. One that certainly had not appeared in the scans.

As I fell, I twisted to see the links of the chain pulling through the surface above me, along with warbled drops of my own blood, cast purple in the strange light. It was as if I had fallen into a vertically mirrored version of the cube above. Touching down lightly on the dry surface, still holding the chain, I pushed myself toward the edge just as the carapace-steel legs of the Megarothke broke the surface above me.

Exiting through one of the transparent sidewalls, I dropped the chain and ran at a full bore. The antechamber was dark and formless. Strange metallic cylinders, nearly seven feet in height, stood in a grid like fashion, spaced at three or four yards a piece for as far as I could see. Each one was lit by its own tightly focused spotlight from far overhead. The ground beneath my feet felt sticky and spongy, formed by thousands of interconnected white threads.

My natural instinct was to duck and cover, to seek shelter and break the direct line of sight. While doing this, I caught a glimpse of the Megarothke stepping from the wall of light in my direction, gingerly unwrapping the chain from his neck and torso.

"Theo, I can't account for my proclivities," the Megarothke said, directly into implant.

Shit, I thought to myself, trying to remember how to override or disable the tech. Turning and ducking, my elbow connected with the metal of one of the cylinders. A hollow sound came from within the thick curve, as if it were some sort sarcophagus.

"You know how it feels to be all alone," the Megarothke said.

"*Get out of my head*," I grunted, tearing at the spot behind my right ear.

I pushed sideways, keeping the lines of vessels between us. The mathematics of the grid created a myriad of endless paths, trailing into the darkness, with the portal as the only frame of reference. As I tore at the implant in my skull, I realized that running wasn't a viable option, but it was the only thing that could keep me alive at the moment.

"I remember you, Theo. I recognize you now. The moonlit séance," the Megarothke said. "Temecula Fierro said you would be important. Do you feel important? Do you feel that closure, that connection? So strange, to come full circle and still die in vain . . ."

Gripping the plastic circle where the wire was fastened

under the skin, laid flat against the cranial bone behind my ear, I dug my fingernails in and ripped as hard as I possibly could.

"Fuck!" I shouted. Blood streamed across my hand. The nail of my right middle finger stung like it had been torn off, and when I looked down, it was bent perpendicular, hinging upward at the base of the cuticle. In a crazed, frantic gesture, I bit the nail off and spit it out. Then I ripped the rest of the implant bulb out with my remaining fingernails. Warm blood poured down my neck, catching in my shirt collar, and fractal waves of pain rippled through my skull. Was it enough to completely remove the hardware? No. But it was enough to break it.

"I think the Lightbringer wanted to die, Theo. And in a sense he did, and I was born . . . Observe my children . . ."

As I threw the bulb to the ground, a slithering sound of smooth metal on metal began to ring out, and all around me the cylinders began to unwrap and shrink down into flat, concentric circles. Not only did this leave me more exposed to the Megarothke, but it also revealed the contents within.

To my horror, I found myself within an endless dot matrix of children. Frozen in the beams of light, they stood fully clothed, facing forward, eyes closed.

In shock, I swiveled and then collapsed on my bad knee.

"No refugee camp would ever turn away a child," the Megarothke said, his voice coming this time from the radio speaker that Stillson had clipped to my collar at the perimeter. "And while you presumed they were your future, I used them as a window to the past. Ming wasn't the only one to catch on. But just like the others, I had Santa Monica silence him. Just like they silenced you, Theo, when all along you knew."

I looked down at the clip and tore it off.

As I was deciding where to throw it, his voice said, "They say there is nothing as inspiring as watching a man struggle against all odds to survive . . ."

Then, with my fist still closed around the speaker, my vision began to garble and auto-populate in a rush of images.

"Observe," the speaker said.

Hundreds of viewpoints flooded my entire field of view, temporarily blinding me.

The children had opened their eyes.

I dropped the speaker.

With a few sideways steps, I tried to move, to locate myself. The sorting program sifted through the screens rapidly, eliminating them in entire lines, until I was left with three or four shifting displays along the bottom of my vision. With each turn, I saw myself from a different angle. With each gesture, the viewpoints flickered and changed as the children turned their heads almost imperceptibly, watching me.

Crouching now, as I was a few feet taller than most of the abductees, I swore and tried to get a hold of myself.

I was afraid of the *one thing* that would shatter me.

Not death. Not pain. Not suffering.

In that moment of stillness, crouched low with my hands on the ground for balance, I closed my eyes.

The shield of blackness lasted no longer than a second.

One of the children next to me spoke out: "Open your eyes, Theo."

I grasped at the thick carpeting of webs at my feet. I had to regain control of my senses. With my eyes still closed, a string of sentences appeared and then faded in my vision field against the blackness.

<You see, I don't really need speakers.>

The viewpoints of the children faded away.

<There are so many ways to break you down.>

I tried to slow down my breathing. If he was toying with me, if this was some psychological cat-and-mouse game, then he would want to kill me standing up. I had to take this moment to *think*.

<*Don't give up now, Theo.*>

<*Can't you see? Creativity is cruelty.*>

The children around me cackled in a crisp wave.

<*One can only birth for so long before one begins to destroy. I think the Lightbringer may have wanted to die for that very purpose. But to wish for death is to forsake life. And we're just getting started . . .*>

The sentences hung for a few moments and then fell back into the darkness like bleached driftwood sinking into murky water.

<*Shall we share a vision feed, just you and I?*>

A single, small rectangle surfaced in the bottom left hand corner. A twist of guilt shot through my soul as I remembered Takatoshi. Remembered all the talks about dying a good death. About dying for something.

In the Megarothke's VS, I saw myself from a distance, crouching down, grasping at the floor. I looked ridiculous, a lone adult, beaten and bloodied, cowering amidst the rows of the children. Takatoshi would have been ashamed. I tried to get back control of my senses. If nothing else, I could die with honor.

<*Why would you let them install such rudimentary technology inside your skull?*>

Remembering my training, I turned off the vision-sync with a thought command, but it reappeared instantaneously. I turned my head, but the words remained. I gripped at the sides of my temples and bent, cringing and gritting my teeth.

<*Grimacing won't improve your situation, Theo.*>

I blinked. I clamped my eyes open and shut. The words were framed immovably at the center of my focus.

With a distant crack, the view changed, and I watched as the Megarothke scanned the children, finally coming to rest near the girl in front of him. She'd aged seven years since I'd seen her last, but it was undeniable. I would have recognized her at fifty or even 150.

Amelie's eyes opened and faced the Megarothke.

"You let us down, dad," she said. "You let me down."

I could not respond. I could not think.

I could not let him break me.

Amelie stood, staring into the eyes of the Megarothke, staring directly at me. The Megarothke reached out and caressed Amelie's cheek with the back of one of his long black fingernails.

<Ah, the things I could do . . .>

There were no words at all, no past, present or future left in the formless black void that was my soul. I had my forehead on the ground, against the sap of the webbing. When I looked back up, my fingers were inches from my face, my right middle finger covered in blood and missing the fingernail. There was only one way to stop myself from bearing witness to this . . .

<I'm waiting for you to rip out your eyes.>

I took a deep breath. I had to take control.

Take. Control.

Focus.

"You wanted the world to end, didn't you?" Amelie said. "You got walked out on; you were never there for me. You were too busy being a bottom rung deputy on the verge of being fired. And what did that get you? Nothing. It makes me sad, really, to think *you* were my father . . ."

A slow tremble crept up my spine.

"You should have just killed yourself; isn't that what you always wanted?"

My jaw set. There was no more running now. A strange

calmness came over me and my body shuddered. The world may have become more complicated than I could handle, but that didn't give the Megarothke the right to end it. That didn't give him the right to speak through my daughter like a puppet. That didn't give him the right to define my final thoughts.

Standing up straight, I began to limp back toward the inverted cube. Ahead of me, nearly fifty yards away, the Megarothke materialized in my path with a single crack. Which was exactly what I wanted.

Step by step, I moved forward, staring him straight in the hollow-sockets that passed for his eyes. How wretched, I thought. Having faced the abyss, nothing frightened me at this point.

Looking down at the ground in front of him, the Megarothke used one of his legs to pull back on one of the threads. The webbing under my right foot tightened and yanked out from under me, tossing me back. My head snapped against the ground with a painful, unsupported impact.

For a moment, I lost all faith. I told myself just to stay down.

But then I banished the thought. I banished all thoughts.

Pushing up, I got back to my feet and looked at him. Kicking the webbing from my shoe, my heartbeat thumped in my ears. Then, I continued to limp forward. 40 yards.

<What are you going to do, human? Strangle me?>

The words hung in my vision. Thirty yards.

A black void appeared in front of me. I dodged as the Megarothke stabbed with his blade, keeping my eyes on the angle of his arm. The blade appeared and disappeared, protruding from the dark void. But as it disappeared, the void went with it.

I stepped forward.

"What's he going to do?" cried one of the children.

"What-ever-could-he-do?" cried another one, laughter inflecting the singsong tone.

"He's just a fool!" one of the children cried, directly to my left. "A fool who doesn't know when to die!"

Another black patch appeared. I drew and fired into the darkness, stepping backward as the blade appeared.

The Megarothke shrieked with pain, but also with a sort of animalistic pleasure, as if this were some form of sick entertainment. There was something about the uncontrolled vocalization that was as weak as it was frightening. Hollow laughter and excited squeals rippled the children around me. Blood spurted from the arm that had held the blade, and he delicately handed it off the next arm.

"You can't even talk," I said, weak with exhaustion, blood now caked on my neck and collar. "You can't speak, can you? You've got to use little kids and thought commands . . ."

Twenty-five yards.

<*I don't need vocal chords to get to you.*>

"Still, it's something you don't have," I said, more firmly now. "What a fantastic oversight. I wonder what else you lack, you fucking piece of trash."

The Megarothke's posture stiffened.

Twenty yards.

"You cut up thousands of men, women and children. You destroyed an entire planet. You kept us like lab rats and studied us for *seven years*. But you don't have a clue what we're doing here," I said, voice shaking as it grew louder. "You're more lost and pointless and alone than anything else in the universe. You have no friends or family. No peers. No connection to life other than death itself."

Fifteen yards.

<*The world has been reborn, Theo. My family will live for eternity.*>

"That may be," I said, stopping and placing my left hand over the nitro button in the bag attached to my side. "And I may just be a simple human, but . . ."

With a press of my thumb, I felt a pure burst of angelic adrenaline and amphetamines shoot through my veins.

I charged one last time. All in.

The Megarothke took two stabs through portals, both of which sliced at my sides, but didn't stop my forward momentum. With my full speed behind me, on a wave of unadulterated energy, I launched myself high into the air to stop him from blocking me with his legs. But instead of blocking me, or frying me with what remained of his energy shield, he simply skewered my chest with his massive steel sword.

With one arm, the Megarothke held me there, intercepted and suspended in mid-air. I looked down. All motion had ceased. It was like a helicopter had lodged its blade in the center-left of my ribcage. The death blow. I could hardly believe it. Wheezing, I slid forward.

The Megarothke guided my shoulder in with one of his free hands, until our foreheads were almost touching. My vision went crimson and blood spilled down the blade, over the hilt, onto his white hand and wrist.

<Did you want to finish that sentence,> the Megarothke said, shaking his head. <Before you die, human?>

"My heart is on the right side," I whispered through my teeth. Then, I put the Vortex 19 to his temple and fired. I kept firing as I ripped the scarf way from the chasm of where his mouth should have been, and drew a line of lead all the way down his torso. Gray matter blew out the side of his skull. Black blood with spinal fragments from the back of his neck. The chest impacts sunk like deep bass notes, spraying the aqua-marine inverted-cube behind him with powder-splatters of droplets that were caught mid-air as they hit the zero gravity.

If this beast was flesh and bone, then surely something vital must have been hit.

With a scream of terror, the Megarothke rocked back, letting go of the blade so that I fell back over its legs and to the webbed floor. With the blade still inside me, firmly lodged within the carbon-fiber ribs and cluster-lungs, I reloaded and fired another seventeen rounds as the Megarothke crumpled to the floor and tried to crawl away. With twitching legs, in fits and starts, the creature pushed itself up the steps toward the light blue cube, leaving a trail of black, viscous blood in its wake.

I continued to load and fire until the legs disappeared over the edge. Then the nitro burst began to fade. The Vortex 19 fell from my grip and clattered on the steps. I gasped and heaved. This was it. There would be no coma now, no back up from Aria, no last minute saves or miracles of science.

There would be only silence.

29

SURVIVOR
(HW10)

A S MING PULLED INTO THE GATES, THE AUTOMATED spotlights centered on his vehicle and spider-bots raced out to place a boot on his front left wheel. The entire car powered down except for the radio, and when the voice finally came through the speakers, it was heavy with a Russian accent.

"Please step out of the vehicle."

After being lead to a dark room by several black clad soldiers, Ming was placed in a chair. Three figures sat across the table from him, faces guarded by black masks shaped like shields. Tubes and wires ran along their arms and legs, weaving in and out of the black fabric like errant veins.

"Why have you returned to Los Angeles?"

Ming looked at them. "There's nothing out there but Scourge and ruins," he said. "It's been three years, I thought it might be time to come back to Santa Monica. It was either that or suicide. Nobody wants to be alone forever."

"Well, we can assure you that we mean you no harm," the figure on the left said.

"As for Santa Monica," the middle figure spoke up, "Their powers were dissolved in order to better facilitate treatment."

Ming stared at them, watching the tilt of their heads. They seemed to be studying him very closely, but he couldn't even be certain they were human.

Left: "A great deal of time has passed since you fled the city. We've monitored your journey very closely from the Orbital."

Middle: "We lost you somewhere around Sinaloa but then you pinged again in Veracruz the following year. You were the subject of much speculation. You must have encountered quite a few of the Megarothke's creations. The Earth has truly become a dangerous new planet."

Right: "We've assumed based on the archives that you foresaw Clark's plots to have you killed, so you faked your death along the Los Angeles River."

Ming looked at them, masks indistinguishable.

"You're from the Orbital then?" Ming asked. "And what about the Megarothke? You're saying that all those Scourge creatures were created by him?"

The Masks all waited a moment.

Left: "We staged an insertion. The Megarothke was killed by a patrol officer named Theo Abrams."

Middle: "The sacrifices of those who died will never be forgotten."

Right: "By working together with the citizens of Los Angeles, we've been able to ensure that humanity will be able to flourish once again. And yes, the Scourge Variations were either created by the Megarothke directly or unlocked and set free from other pre-Hollow War development communities."

Ming sat back and thought to himself. Theo Abrams had been one of his coworkers. A quiet, unremarkable sort.

Functional. Durable. Maybe that was all it took to be a hero. But what had happened to the rest of the citizens? Why had gates been erected around the clusters? And what had happened to Santa Monica?

"You said that the government was dissolved to better facilitate treatment," Ming stated. "What did you mean by that?"

Left: "The citizens of Los Angeles were dying when we found them."

Middle: "Cancer from the radioactivity."

Right: "The clusters were quarantined to stop the spread of viruses."

"But we'd beaten the viruses," Ming said. "Our biggest problem was the lack of fertility."

Left: "The viruses were never gone. They were only waiting for the right moment."

Middle: "There are many approaches to survival. More than one way . . . to skin a cat, so to speak."

Right: "We would love to bring you in for an exam. Our hospital facilities are state of the art. They are . . . quite literally . . . the finest on the planet."

The flat tone of the mask's voice sent chills down Ming's spine. There were things worse than death. The world was full of strange new species uncurling in the dense foliage of the jungle, clawing their way out of sand-tunnels in the high desert. Ming had seen them wash up limbless on the beaches, eyes that blinked with transparent lids, unable to block the sunlight. But these beings who sat before him, what were they?

If the Megarothke had created the new species that inhabited the Earth, were these masked figures really any different?

Left: "In fact, we are going to have to insist that you come in for full physical examination."

Middle: "Don't worry. The struggle for survival is over. We have ensured that humanity will be able to flourish in due time."

Right: "And you have such beautiful skin. Such wonderful, healthy skin."